The Boxcar Children Mysteries

THE BOXCAR CHILDREN
WINTER SPECIAL

THE MYSTERY IN THE SNOW

THE MYSTERY ON BLIZZARD MOUNTAIN

THE MYSTERY AT SNOWFLAKE INN

created by
GERTRUDE CHANDLER WARNER

ALBERT WHITMAN & Company
Chicago, Illinois

The Boxcar Children Winter Special
created by Gertrude Chandler Warner.

ISBN 10: 0-8075-0886-1
ISBN 13: 978-0-8075-0886-2

For more information about Albert Whitman & Company,
please visit our web site at www.albertwhitman.com.

Contents

THE MYSTERY IN THE SNOW

created by

GERTRUDE CHANDLER WARNER

Illustrated by Charles Tang

ALBERT WHITMAN & Company
Chicago, Illinois

The Mystery In the Snow
created by Gertrude Chandler Warner;
illustrated by Charles Tang.

ISBN 10: 0-8075-5393-X
ISBN 13: 978-0-8075-5393-0

For more information about Albert Whitman & Company,
please visit our web site at www.albertwhitman.com.

Contents

CHAPTER 1

Grandfather's Surprise

Benny glanced out the window over the kitchen counter. Outside, his twelve-year-old sister, Jessie, was playing with their dog, Watch. Snowflakes fell onto the Aldens' back lawn.

"I hope it snows all day," six-year-old Benny said. "And all night!" He dropped the last spoonful of dough onto a cookie sheet.

At the table, his sister Violet, who was ten years old, was sprinkling powdered sugar on a freshly baked batch of golden cookies. "It would be nice to have lots of snow," she said. "We could go sledding."

"And build snowmen," Benny added.

Mrs. McGregor, the Aldens' housekeeper, carried Benny's filled cookie sheet to the oven. "I don't think there's much chance of that," she said. "A few flurries is all those clouds have in them."

Benny sighed. He had been looking forward to the season's first big snowfall. It was late this year. "It won't be much of a winter vacation without snow," he said.

"Let's make our own snow," Violet suggested.

Benny turned away from the window. "How?" he asked.

"We'll cut snowflakes," Violet told him.

Benny knew how to do that. Before vacation, he and the other first-graders had made paper snowflakes to decorate their classroom. "I thought you meant *real* snow," he said, disappointment in his voice.

"We'll hang them in the window, Benny," Violet said. "That way, every time you look out, you'll see snow."

"What a good idea," Mrs. McGregor said.

"And if you make some small snowflakes — no bigger around than the cookies, I'll show you something else you can do."

Benny was curious. He cut the paper into four pieces. Then he folded and refolded each section. In one piece, he cut several small holes. Each was a different shape. When he unfolded the paper, he had a beautiful snowflake.

Mrs. McGregor laid it on top of a cookie.

Violet's eyes lit up. "Talk about good ideas!" she said.

Benny didn't think it was such a good idea. "Who's going to eat cookies with paper snowflakes on them?" he asked.

Mrs. McGregor laughed. "Oh, I think everyone will eat these when we're finished."

Violet sprinkled the powdered sugar over the snowflake. Then she carefully removed the paper. The top of the cookie was dusted with a beautiful white design.

The three of them cut more paper designs.

"Can I sprinkle the sugar?" Benny asked.

Violet handed him the can. Benny turned it upside down and shook hard. The sugar

poured through the holes in the can top like snow from a cloud.

Just then, Jessie opened the door and Watch bolted through. He slid across the floor to the table. Sniffing the air, he sat back on his hind legs and begged. Benny slipped him a cookie.

Jessie hung her coat on the hall tree beside the door. "It sure smells good in here," she said.

Henry, their fourteen-year-old brother, came in with an armload of firewood.

"Is it still snowing?" Violet asked.

Henry set the firewood down near the kitchen fireplace. "It's stopped," he said. "At least *out*side. Looks like a regular snowstorm in here."

Benny laughed. "It's the sugar," he said. "We're using it to make our own snow."

Grandfather Alden entered from the front of the house. He was wearing his overcoat and scarf. His cheeks were rosy and his eyes sparkled. It was early for him to be home. He rarely left his mill until the end of the workday.

"Grandfather!" Benny exclaimed. "What a surprise!"

"Did I hear something about snow when I came in?" Mr. Alden asked.

"We were hoping for a snowstorm," Violet told him.

Grandfather smiled. He looked as though he had a big secret. "What if I said that you'd see more snow this week than you've seen in a very long time?"

"Where?" they all asked at once.

Mr. Alden told them about his friend, Todd Mercer, who owned a lodge in the hills two hours north of Greenfield. "It's a wonderful place," he said. "Every winter holiday, there's a kind of carnival with special events and prizes. Todd's been wanting me to bring you children up there since he bought the lodge."

"Well, then, why haven't you, Grandfather?" Benny asked.

Mr. Alden chuckled. "That's exactly the question I asked myself this morning," he said. "So I phoned Todd."

Benny couldn't stand the suspense. He

shot to his feet. "Are we going?" he asked.

Grandfather looked from one to the other. "Do you want to go?"

They all said, "Yes!"

"When will we leave, Grandfather?" Jessie asked. She was thinking about the packing that would have to be done.

"Do you think you could be ready in" — Mr. Alden looked at his watch — "an hour?"

The children glanced at one another.

Henry wondered if his skis needed waxing.

Jessie wondered if her skates would fit.

Violet wondered where she had put her winter hat — the one with the purple stripes.

Benny wondered what food they would take.

There was so much to do. How could they possibly be ready in an hour? They looked at Grandfather Alden.

"Yes!" they all said. "We'll be ready!"

CHAPTER 2

Missing Keys

Benny was the first to see the carved wooden sign. It read *Snow Haven Lodge*. "We're here!" he exclaimed.

Mr. Alden turned the station wagon into the long driveway. Snowflakes danced in the headlights. "And not a moment too soon," he said. "With all this snow, driving will be impossible before too long."

Violet glanced out her window. The branches of the evergreens were already heavy with snow. The ground below was covered in a soft blanket of white. "It's so beautiful!" she said.

"And so quiet," Jessie said.

"What's that up ahead, Grandfather?" Henry asked. He pointed toward a long, low building. Its lights cast a warm glow through the gathering dusk.

"Must be the lodge," Mr. Alden told him.

"Is that where we'll stay?" Jessie asked.

"I imagine so," Mr. Alden answered.

"I'd rather stay in one of those," Benny said. He pointed to a group of small cabins on their right.

Grandfather stopped the car in front of the lodge. Several other cars were parked there. Watch sat up and wagged his short tail.

They climbed out of the station wagon and headed inside. A fire blazed in the large, stone fireplace. Big, comfortable couches and chairs were grouped on the wood floor. Here and there, small clusters of people talked and laughed.

"James!" A tall, thin man stepped out from behind a counter and came toward them.

Mr. Alden grabbed the man's hand. "Todd, it's good to see you."

Todd Mercer smiled. "I'm glad you made it before the storm," he said.

"So are we!" Benny piped up.

"This must be the famous Benny," Mr. Mercer said.

Benny blushed. He'd never been called *famous* before. It made him speechless.

Mr. Alden introduced his other grandchildren, and Watch, who had followed them inside. "I hope it's all right for our dog to be inside the lodge. He's very well-behaved," said Mr. Alden.

"Fine with me," Mr. Mercer said.

The door opened and a gust of snow blew in. A man and woman dressed in ski suits rushed inside. A rosy-cheeked boy about Henry's age tagged along after them.

"James, why don't you sign in," Mr. Mercer said to Mr. Alden. He turned to the children. "Help yourselves to the hot chocolate and snacks on that table over there." He pointed toward the windows.

Benny's eyes widened when he saw the

table covered with plates of cookies and small sandwiches, and a large, steaming pot of hot chocolate. "What a sight!" he said.

Jessie looked out the windows. Children skated on the pond behind the lodge. Snow fell all around them. "It looks like a picture in a storybook," she said.

"Better," Benny said. "You can't *eat* pictures." He helped himself to a cookie.

Violet laughed. "Oh, Benny," she said. "Jessie was talking about the view."

Benny glanced out the window. "That's nice, too, but — "

"You can't eat it," Henry finished.

They carried their snacks to the couch.

Mr. Mercer brought over the young boy who'd just arrived. "I want you to meet Jimmy Phelps," he said. "He's been with us every winter vacation since he was no bigger than you, Benny."

Jimmy smiled shyly. "Hi," he said.

Henry moved over. "Sit down here," he said. "There's plenty of room."

"Get some food first," Benny suggested. "It's delicious."

Jimmy nodded. "Okay," he said. "And I have to sign in." He went to the high desk and signed the guest book.

Jimmy's parents and Mr. Mercer were talking to Grandfather.

"I wonder if Mr. and Mrs. Phelps are staying here, too," Jessie said.

"Why wouldn't they?" Henry asked.

Jessie shrugged. "Mr. Mercer said Jimmy's been here every winter; he didn't say anything about his parents."

Benny looked at the grown-ups. "Maybe they're not his parents," he said. Just then, Jimmy returned. "Are those people your parents?" Benny asked him.

Jimmy nodded. "Yes," he answered. "Why?"

"Benny asks lots of questions," Henry explained.

"That's the only way to get answers," Benny defended himself.

Everyone laughed.

"Are they staying here, too?" Jessie asked Jimmy.

Jimmy glanced toward his parents. "No,"

he said. "They never stay." He looked glumly at his feet.

"Why not?" Violet asked. "It's such a nice place."

Before he could answer, someone called, "Jimmy!"

Jimmy popped to his feet. "Freddy!"

A girl rushed up. "I am so glad to see you," she said. "I was afraid you wouldn't be here this year."

"Freddy, meet the Aldens," Jimmy said.

"Freddy?" Benny said. "Isn't that a boy's name?"

The girl took off her green knit cap. Her short, black hair curled tightly around her face. "My name's actually Frederica," she said. "Freddy's easier."

"That's for sure," Benny agreed.

Mr. and Mrs. Phelps joined the group.

"Jimmy, we're about ready to go," Mr. Phelps said.

Mrs. Phelps hugged her son. "You're sure you have everything?"

Jimmy sighed. "Mom, how many times did we check?"

"You'll call us if you need anything?" she said.

Mr. Phelps took her arm. "Come on, Grace. With this snow, it'll take us a while to get to the airport." He put his arm around Jimmy. "Walk us out to the car, son," he said.

Freddy watched them leave. When they had gone outside, she said, "They don't know what they're missing."

"Are your parents here?" Jessie asked.

She shook her head. "They went to visit my sister. She moved to Florida last summer. But they'll be here later — for the awards dinner."

"Why didn't you go with them?" Violet wanted to know.

"And miss the snow and the fun here? No way," Freddy said. "Besides, Jimmy and I are team captains this year." She leaned close as though she were about to share a secret. "My team's going to win." She giggled with excitement. "It's going to be the best year ever."

"It'll certainly be the biggest year," Mr.

Mercer said as he came up beside them. "Seems I've overbooked the lodge."

At his side, Grandfather said, "Todd's looking for volunteers to stay in one of those cabins we saw on the way in."

"Anyone interested?" Mr. Mercer asked.

Five hands shot up. Two of them belonged to Benny.

When Jimmy returned, Mr. Mercer called to him. "Jimmy," he said, "I left the team box in the equipment shop. Would you mind getting it? You know where the keys are."

"On the board behind the desk?" Jimmy asked to make sure.

Mr. Mercer nodded.

Jimmy hurried off.

"What's the team box?" Henry asked.

"Everyone signs a card and puts it in the box," Freddy explained. "Tomorrow morning, Jimmy and I will pick names out of it. That's the way we form the teams. Then we have five contests: skiing, sledding, skating, snow sculpting and ice carving."

"Mr. Mercer, I can't find the keys," Jimmy called.

Mr. Mercer went over to help him. The Aldens followed.

Mr. Mercer stepped behind the desk. He looked through the keys hanging on the board. Each one had a tag. "That's strange," he said. "The keys were here earlier today. I put them here myself."

"Maybe they fell on the floor," Jimmy suggested.

Everyone looked around, but no one saw the keys. Mr. Mercer looked upset.

"Couldn't you use another box?" Benny suggested.

"Yes," Mr. Mercer answered, "but we have to be able to get into the equipment shop."

"There're all kinds of things in there we need," Freddy added.

"Without them," Jimmy said, "we won't be able to have the games."

"It will make things very difficult." Mr. Mercer paused a moment. Then, looking around at the concerned faces of all the children he said, "I'm sure they'll turn up *somewhere*."

CHAPTER 3

Their Own Little Cabin

After a supper of spaghetti and salad in the lodge dining room, Grandfather drove the children to the cabin.

"This is as close as we can get," he said as he stopped the station wagon.

"We're close enough," Jessie said. "From what Mr. Mercer told me, that's our cabin just over there."

Their log house stood out from the others. It was the only one with a light on.

Everyone hopped out of the car. Watch ran, his nose to the ground. Henry unhooked

the skis from the car's roof. Jessie gathered the skates from the back. Violet, Benny, and Mr. Alden carried the children's suitcases to the cabin. When Grandfather opened the door they all saw a fire dancing in the small stone fireplace with a sofa and two over-stuffed chairs clustered around it. At the end of the room, near a small kitchen, stood a bare table and six plain chairs.

Jessie and Henry came in. They looked around for a place to put their skis and skates. Henry noticed a long wooden board on the wall beside the door.

"This rack must be made for skis," he said. He slipped his skis between two of the metal bands on the board.

"There are pegs here, too," Jessie said. "A perfect place to hang our skates."

"And there's still room for our coats," Violet said as she slipped out of her purple jacket.

They all took off their coats and boots while Grandfather looked around the cabin. He found two small bedrooms, each with bunk beds and a large chest of drawers.

"The beds aren't made," he said when he returned to the main room, "but there are plenty of sheets and blankets in the dresser drawers."

"We'll find everything, Grandfather," Jessie assured him. She knew he wanted to get back to the lodge to visit with Mr. Mercer.

"All right then," Mr. Alden said, "I'll be on my way."

He opened the door and Watch darted in. His nose and whiskers were all white, and snow hung from his chin like a beard. He ran around the room smelling everything, leaving little puddles of melting snow wherever his nose touched.

The Aldens waved to their grandfather. Then, Henry closed and latched the door.

"Benny and I will share one bedroom," he said. "You girls take the other."

"I get the top bunk," Benny said.

"Fine with me," Henry agreed.

Benny unzipped his duffel bag. He pulled out a white box. "What should we do with this?" he asked.

"What's in it?" Jessie asked.

"The cookies we made this morning," Benny answered.

Jessie looked around the room. There was a small sink near the table. Above it was a cabinet. She opened its door. "Put them in here, Benny," she said.

Benny handed her the box. He wasn't tall enough to reach the shelf.

"There're dishes in here and paper napkins. And, look! Here's a tablecloth," Jessie said.

"Let's cover the table," Violet suggested. "It'll look more homey."

Jessie took out the red-and-white checked cloth and laid it on the tabletop.

"Now all we need's a centerpiece," Violet said.

Benny dragged his duffel bag across the room. "How about some fruit?" He put several apples and oranges on the table.

"Here's a container," Henry said. He slipped a basket off a peg beside the fireplace.

Violet arranged the fruit in the round basket and placed it in the center of the table.

Then, Benny said, "Let's eat."

"We just had supper," Henry reminded him.

"I know, but I'm getting sleepy," Benny said, "and I can't go to bed without a snack."

Jessie took down the box of cookies. "I don't suppose a cookie or two would hurt," she said.

"Too bad we don't have something to drink," Violet said.

Benny pulled several cans of juice from his bag. "Ta-da," he said.

Henry laughed. Then, he took four cups from the cabinet shelf.

"I don't need a cup," Benny told him as he fished in the duffel. "I brought my own." He held up the cracked pink cup he had found in a dump when they had lived in the boxcar.

Jessie gave each of them two cookies on a red paper napkin.

Henry poured the juice.

"The juice is warm," Benny said. "I like it cold."

"I can fix that," Henry said. He took a bowl from the cabinet and went outside. He returned with a bowlful of snow.

Benny scooped some into his cup. "It's like a snowcone without the cone," he said.

They began talking about the next day's activities.

"Whose team will we be on?" Violet wondered aloud.

"Maybe we'll be on different teams," Jessie said.

"I want to be on Freddy's team," Benny said.

"Why?" Violet asked. "Jimmy'll be a good captain, too."

"But Freddy said her team was going to win," Benny reminded his sister.

"Just because she says it, doesn't make it so," Jessie argued.

"I don't care who wins," Violet said. "Just being a part of a team will be fun."

"There might not be any teams," Henry said.

They remembered the locked equipment shop.

"What do you suppose happened to the keys?" Jessie asked.

"Maybe someone took them," Benny said.

"Why would anyone do that?" Henry asked.

They could not think of a single reason.

"Maybe Mr. Mercer put them somewhere else and forgot," Violet suggested.

"Let's hope he finds them," Jessie said.

"Or figures out some other way to get into the equipment shop," Henry put in.

Benny shivered with excitement. "I can't wait to find out whose team I'll be on," he said.

They decided to make up their beds and go to sleep. That way, morning would come faster.

CHAPTER 4

Flat Tires

The next morning, the Aldens met Jimmy Phelps in front of the lodge. He was taking off his skates.

"Is breakfast over already?" Benny asked him. He couldn't imagine anyone doing too much before eating.

"No," Jimmy answered. "I was just working up an appetite."

"I'm glad I don't have to do that!" Benny commented.

"Benny likes to eat," Jessie explained.

Jimmy smiled. His rosy cheeks became

even rounder. "I figured that," he said.

On their way into the lounge, Henry asked, "Did Mr. Mercer find the keys?"

Jimmy shook his head. "No," he said. "I don't know what he'll do."

Mr. Mercer stood just inside the door. He pointed to a table near the entrance. "Sign your names on those cards," he said, "and put them into that big box."

"Is that the box from the equipment shop?" Jessie asked.

Mr. Mercer shook his head. "No, the equipment shop is still locked. I'm going into town later to get a locksmith. He can make new keys."

"We thought you might have to call off the games," Henry said.

"Well, it is a problem not being able to get into the equipment shop. But, I'd never call off the games. Not for a little thing like a missing key," Mr. Mercer assured them.

The Aldens went over to fill out the cards.

Their grandfather got up from his chair near the fire. "Good morning," he called out.

"Good morning, Grandfather," the children responded.

Freddy came in, pulling off her green knit hat. She was wearing a one piece ski outfit that was bright green, orange, and yellow. And she had on gloves to match!

"Did everybody sign up?" she called. "I want you all to have a chance to be on my team."

Several children who hadn't filled out the cards formed a line behind the Aldens. Everyone else headed for the dining room. Long tables were set with red-and-white checked tablecloths. At the front of the large, sunlit room, the longest table was filled with food: egg dishes, bacon, sausage, rolls, toast, pancakes, fruit, three kinds of juice, milk, coffee, tea — something for every taste.

"Everything looks so good," Jessie commented. "It's hard to know what to choose."

Benny took a plate from the stack at the end of the table. "Take some of everything," he advised his sister. "That way you won't have to make hard decisions."

Grandfather chose a toasted English muffin and a bowl of fruit; the younger Aldens took Benny's advice.

After breakfast, Mr. Mercer went to the front of the room. Jimmy and Freddy followed with the box of names.

"Attention, everyone," the man said. "It's time to pick teams. Freddy and Jimmy are our team captains. As your name is called, please come up and join your leader."

Everyone started talking excitedly.

Mr. Mercer hushed them. "I have to go into town to the locksmith," he said. "So I'll let your team captains take over." He left the room.

Freddy reached into the box and pulled out a card. "Danny Cahill," she read.

In the far corner of the room, a red-headed boy, about Benny's age, stood up. He walked slowly to the front of the room.

Freddy greeted him with a broad smile. "Welcome to the winning team, Danny," she said.

Jimmy picked out a name. He read it to himself; then looked up. He had a funny expression on his face. It was hard to tell whether he was happy about his choice, or sad. "Beth Markham," he announced. "Last year's top skater."

Beth skipped to the front of the room, her ponytail swinging.

Two more team members were chosen.

Benny wiggled in his chair. "I can't stand the suspense," he whispered.

Henry was the first of the Aldens chosen. He would be on Jimmy's team. Jessie and then Violet were picked for that team, too.

Benny glanced around the room. He and an older girl were the only ones whose names hadn't been called.

It was Jimmy's turn. "There are only two names left," he said.

Benny leaned forward in his chair. "Hurry, hurry, hurry," he urged silently.

Jimmy reached into the box. He drew out a card. He looked at it. He even turned it over.

Benny couldn't sit still. He popped to his feet. "Hurry, hurry, hurry," he repeated, but this time, he said the words aloud.

Everyone laughed. Benny was so embarrassed he sat down again.

Finally, Jimmy said, "And the last member of our team is . . . Benny Alden!"

His new teammates cheered.

Freddy called the last name, "Nan Foster!" and that team cheered as a short girl, who looked like she was about ten years old, slowly walked up. She seemed to be the only person in the room who wasn't smiling.

Just then, Mr. Mercer appeared in the doorway, looking grim. "You're not going to believe this," he said.

"What happened?" Grandfather Alden asked.

"It's my truck. The tires are flat," he responded with disbelief. "All four of them!"

CHAPTER 5

A New Mystery

Mr. Mercer was upset. "I parked the truck out by the skating rink last night. The tires were fine then."

"*One* flat tire I could understand," Grandfather said. "But *four*?"

"That sounds like it was intentional," Henry pointed out.

"But who would do something like that? And why?" said Mr. Mercer.

"First missing keys and now flat tires. Do you suppose they're connected?" Henry wondered aloud.

"Probably not," Jessie said.

"Todd, do you have an air pump?" Mr. Alden asked.

Mr. Mercer shook his head. "It's broken," he said. "I've been meaning to get another one."

Grandfather offered to drive him into town. "We'll get a pump *and* go to the locksmith," he said.

Mr. Mercer agreed, and he and Grandfather hurried to Grandfather's car.

Freddy said, "We'll go on with the tryouts."

"There are five events," Jimmy said. "Skating, skiing, sledding, snow sculpting, and ice carving."

An excited murmur shot through the group.

"Snow sculpting?" Benny whispered to Violet. "Is that like making snowmen?"

Violet nodded. "I think so."

"Then, I'll try out for that," he said. He wondered what he would have to do. He raised his hand. "How do you try out for snow sculpting?" he asked.

"You can't," Freddy told him. "That and ice carving — if you want to do one of those, just sign up."

"And you can sign up for as many events as you want," Jimmy added.

A boy about Jessie's age stood up. He tossed his head to get his long, straight hair out of his eyes. "What if you want to try out for, say, skiing, but you don't have skis?"

"You'll find everything you need at the equipment shop, Matt," Freddy told him.

"If and when Mr. Mercer gets it open," Jimmy said.

"What if you don't want to sign up for anything?" Nan Foster asked.

Freddy stared at her. She seemed so surprised by the question that she didn't have an answer.

A boy named Pete, who was sitting next to Nan, rolled his eyes. "We can't win with people like her on our team," he scoffed.

Nan looked as though she might cry.

"It's okay," Jimmy said to her. "Sometimes, people try out for an event, and they don't make it. That's okay, too. They get to be assistants. We need everybody."

Beth smiled at Nan. "You should try out for something, though. It's fun," she said.

"Where do we try out?" Henry asked.

"The skating tryouts are in an hour, at the pond. Right afterward we'll have skiing on the slopes, and then sledding on the smaller hill." Jimmy held up two pieces of yellow lined paper. "Here are the sign-up sheets." He looked around to be sure there were no other questions. "That's it!"

"Yea, team!" Freddy said.

"What're you going to try out for, Henry?" Jessie asked.

"Skiing," Henry answered.

"Anything else?"

"Maybe sledding."

"I'm signing up for ice carving," Violet said. "How about you, Jessie?"

"Skating, for sure," Jessie answered.

"I'm trying out for everything," Benny said.

Henry laughed. "This isn't food, Benny," he teased.

They got in line to sign up.

Violet was behind Nan. "Oh, Nan," she said, "you changed your mind about trying out."

Nan lowered her eyes. "No, I didn't," she said.

Violet was confused. "But . . . you're standing in line."

"I don't want my parents to know," she explained. "They'd be upset. They want me to have fun."

"Don't *you* want to have fun?" Violet asked.

The girl shrugged. "I never have fun," she answered.

Violet thought about that. She tried to imagine what it would be like not to enjoy herself. No matter where she went or what she did, she expected to have a good time. And she always did.

It was Nan's turn to sign up. Twisting the ends of her red knit scarf, she stared at the paper on the table.

Violet stepped up beside her. She picked up two pencils. "Here," she said and gave Nan one. "Let's both sign up for ice carving.

You don't have to try out for that."

Nan looked discouraged. "I don't know anything about ice carving," she said. "I wouldn't want to be the one who loses for the whole team."

"I don't know a thing about it either," Violet assured her. "Maybe we could help each other."

Nan brightened. Then, just as suddenly, her round face clouded. "We're on different teams," she said.

Violet had forgotten that. Because of her brothers and sister, she usually thought about cooperation, not competition. "That won't matter," she said. "It'll be a help just knowing each other. I mean, neither of us knows what we're doing; that makes us equal."

Nan smiled for the first time. "Then, your team'd have an equal chance of losing."

Although Violet wouldn't have put it that way, she agreed.

Nan signed her name on the yellow sheet that read ICE CARVING. "Thanks," she said and hurried off.

When they had all signed up, the children headed back to the cabin to get their skates and skis. Outside, the snow reflected the sunlight.

Henry fished a pair of sunglasses out of his jacket pocket. "It's really bright," he commented.

"I like the way the snow sparkles in places," Violet said.

Benny said, "I like the way it sounds when you walk on it. *Scrunch, scrunch, scrunch.*"

Jessie sighed. She liked everything about the snow. It even made the air smell fresher. "It'll be a good week," she said.

They walked along in silence, each thinking about all that had happened since they had arrived at the lodge.

Finally, Henry said, "You know, I think the missing keys and the flat tires are connected somehow."

"That means we have a mystery," Jessie said.

"I hope you're wrong, Jessie," Benny said. "We'll be too busy to solve one!"

CHAPTER 6

The Tryouts

A little while later, Benny sat on a bench at the edge of the skating pond. He was trying to lace up his skates. His hands were clumsy inside his gloves. When he took his gloves off, his fingers got too cold. "I'll never get these laces tight enough," he complained aloud.

Jessie was already skating. Henry and Violet had gone to look at the ski run. Benny sighed. There was no one to help him.

From the next bench, an older boy called, "Having trouble?"

It was Matt, the boy with the hair in his eyes. But now, his hair was off his face, held back by a wide black headband.

"It's these laces," Benny said.

Matt walked over on his racing skates. "Here, let me help," he said. Then he bent down and carefully laced up Benny's skates.

"I think these skates may be too small for you," he said.

Benny was surprised. "They fit last year."

Matt laughed. "Well, maybe they shrank," he teased.

"Skates don't shrink," Benny said.

"No, but feet grow."

Benny laughed. "Oh," he said. "I forgot about that."

"You can get a bigger pair at the equipment shop when Mr. Mercer gets new keys," Matt told him. Then, he sped off.

Benny looked at the skaters. Jessie was practicing her forward crossovers. Beth was doing jumps. Jimmy was skating backward. All the people on the ice were excellent skaters. Benny was good, but not that good. He decided not to try out for skating.

Violet and Henry came back in time for the tryouts. Many of the adults came out to the rink to watch the six skaters. Mr. Alden strolled up to the children. He had just returned from driving Mr. Mercer to town.

"The locksmith is making the new keys," he said. "The equipment shop will be open in time for the ski tryouts."

Jimmy put his skaters through their paces quickly. Matt was the best racer; Jessie and Beth the best figure skaters.

Freddy and her group came along. They sat on a bench near the Aldens to put on their skates. Freddy watched Jimmy's skaters carefully. She saw every turn, every pivot, every jump. She did not smile.

"Freddy doesn't look very happy," Benny observed.

Finally, Jimmy was ready to announce his choices. The skaters formed a circle around him.

"Beth, Matt, Jessie, and me." Jimmy pointed to each as he called out their names. To the two losers, he said, "You're both very good. If I could choose more than four skaters, you would have made it, too."

The Aldens admired his kindness.

"Now, there's a good leader," Mr. Alden said.

Jessie skated over.

Everyone congratulated her.

"The ice makes it easy to skate well," she said. "It's smooth as glass."

Freddy stepped onto the ice. "Come on," she said to her group. "Let's show them some real skating." But she still didn't smile.

Grandfather went back to the lodge to warm up. Most of the other adults decided to do that, too.

Jimmy headed for the ski hill. His team trekked along beside him.

"Have you been captain before?" Henry asked.

Jimmy shook his head. "No, this is the first time."

"Do your parents know you're captain?" Jessie asked.

Jimmy looked at her in a strange way. "Why do you want to know?" he asked.

Jessie sensed that she had asked the wrong

question. "Oh, no reason. I just thought if they knew . . ." her voice trailed off.

"I'd want them to be here if I were captain," Benny said.

Jimmy didn't respond.

"Don't you miss them?" Benny persisted. "I miss Grandfather when we're away from him."

Jimmy picked up his pace. "It's only for a week," he said. "And, besides, I like being on my own. Especially here. Who wants parents watching every move you make?"

The Aldens were surprised by his harsh tone. Jimmy had seemed so gentle.

After a brief silence, he added, "Don't get me wrong. My parents are terrific. It's just that they can be . . . overprotective sometimes." His voice had lost its sharp edges.

They came to the ski hill. The run started high above them and ended near a long, low, log building.

"Wow!" Benny exclaimed. "That's no hill! It's a mountain."

"It looks like great skiing," Henry commented.

Jimmy shrugged. "It's not bad, but it's nothing compared to the runs in Colorado. That's where my parents are."

"How do you get to the top?" Benny asked.

"Rope tow," Jimmy said. He pointed to a rope moving slowly up the incline.

To Benny, it looked like a moving snake. He trudged along behind his brother toward the log building. It housed the equipment shop and a warming room.

Mr. Mercer was just leaving. "The equipment shop is open," he said.

People clumped across the wooden floor in colorful plastic boots. Dressed in ski clothes and goggles, they looked like moon walkers — only clumsier.

Benny doubted he could walk in the boots, let alone ski. "I don't think I'll try out for skiing," he said.

"That's a good decision," Henry told him. "It's a tough run for a beginner."

"But I would like to try it," Benny said.

"Maybe you could take a lesson," Henry said, changing into his boots. "See you later."

"Good luck!" Benny called out.

Henry went outside. There he snapped on his skis and glided toward the other skiers.

Benny joined his sisters near the windows in the warming house.

"Did you change your mind about trying out?" Jessie asked.

Benny nodded. "I need my energy for snow sculpting."

Violet held up the book she was reading. "You might want to look at this," she said. "It's tells all about ice carving and snow sculpting. I found it in the equipment shop."

"I know how to build snowmen," Benny said.

"But you can build all kinds of other things, too," Violet told him. "It doesn't have to be a snowman."

Benny sat down beside her to look at the book. There were lots of photographs and instructions. You could make lions, dragons, castles — anything. "I still think I'll build a snowman," he said.

They all moved closer to the windows to watch Henry coming down the slope. From this distance, the skiers looked like small, dark shapes. It wasn't long, though, before they spotted Henry. In his bright red ski jacket, he led the pack.

The Aldens weren't surprised when their big brother came inside all smiles, saying, "I made it!"

The sledding tryouts were held on a smaller hill. Everyone who tried out made it. Benny and some of the younger team members would use round plastic sleds. Henry and the other older children would be on toboggans.

That decided, Jimmy said it was time for lunch.

Benny wasn't the only one who was happy to hear that.

CHAPTER 7

The Competition Begins

The Aldens had just sat down to eat when Pete burst into the dining room. He was wearing large orange boots. Their thick rubber soles left a line of snow stars on the floor as he stormed along.

Freddy followed after him. She pulled off her orange, green, and yellow gloves and stuffed them into her pockets. "Pete, listen to me," she said. "You can be timekeeper. That's an important job."

Pete rolled his eyes. "I don't want to be

timekeeper!" he shouted. "I don't want to be anything!" He stormed off.

Jimmy came along carrying his lunch tray. "What's the matter with Pete?" he asked Freddy.

"He didn't make the events he wanted." She moved close to Jimmy and lowered her voice. "This whole thing — it's not fair," she hissed. "You got all the good people. Something has to be done. Something to . . . even things out."

She noticed the Aldens watching her. She turned to them and smiled. "Oh, hi," she said, her tone bright. "I was just telling Jimmy that next year, we'll have to divide up families. It's not fair that one team gets all that talent." She sailed off toward the buffet table.

Jimmy sat down. "We do have a good team," he said. "We could win."

"Are your parents coming for the awards dinner?" Benny asked.

Jimmy's entire face turned red as his cheeks. "The awards dinner? I — uh — "

"Freddy told us about it," Henry said.

"She told us her parents were coming," Benny said. "Will yours be here?"

Jimmy stood up abruptly. "They wouldn't miss it," he said. He took his tray and moved on.

"I wonder why he rushed off like that?" Violet said.

"Maybe he didn't want to talk about the awards dinner," Henry said.

"Why wouldn't he?" Jessie wondered.

Henry shrugged. "The competition hasn't even started. Maybe he thinks it's bad luck to talk about awards so soon."

"Pete and Freddy seemed upset, too," Violet reminded them.

"I'm not sure I like this competition business," Benny said. "It makes everybody act funny."

"You can't think about competing," Jessie told him. "Just think about doing the best you can."

After lunch, Benny met with the other sculptors out on the lawn in front of the lodge. They were all about the same age. The only things they had made with snow were balls, forts, and people.

"We should stick to something that's not too hard," Benny decided.

The others — Jason, Alan, and Debbie — agreed. They would build snowpeople. But what kind?

"Why not do *us*?" Alan asked. "We could have them — us — working on a snow sculpture."

"That's a great idea!" Benny said.

Violet's ice carving group — Violet, Beth, and David — were meeting near the ski slope. No one had ever carved ice before. They were all afraid they couldn't do it.

"It will have to be a simple shape," Beth said.

Watch ambled over to the group. He yawned and put his head in Violet's lap. That gave her an idea.

"How about a dog?" she asked. "We could use Watch as a model."

Beth twisted her pony tail around her fingers. "The legs would be hard to carve," she said.

Violet thought about that. Then, she said, "We won't have to worry about the back legs if we're making him sit."

At the sound of the word *sit*, Watch perked up his ears. Then, he sat.

Everyone laughed.

Benny and his group were having problems. They tried rolling the snow into bigger and bigger balls, but chunks kept falling off.

"The snow's too powdery," Jason complained.

Benny had an idea. "If we had some pans, we could fill them with water and pour it on the snow," he said. "That'd make it easy to pack."

They got four buckets of water from the kitchen. Then, they poured the water on the snow. At first, it seemed as though Benny's plan would work. But the water went fast.

Jason sighed. "We can't keep going all the way back to the kitchen."

"Even if we had enough water," Alan said, "the snow would be too heavy to roll."

"Then we'll have to find some other

way to build," Debbie said.

"Like what?" Jason asked.

Benny remembered a picture he had seen in the snow-sculpting book. "If we had some sticks or something, we could build forms," he said.

Alan liked the idea. "It'll be easy to pack the snow around them," he said.

They looked for something to use to make forms. Behind the lodge, they found a scrap heap next to the garage. Debbie saw an old sled under a tarpaulin. They piled it with metal pipes and strips of wood.

"Take that wire, too," Benny said. "It's perfect for holding the form together."

Now that they knew what they were doing, the work went fast. In an hour, four stick figures stood in the snow. By supper time, they had the rough beginnings of snowy self-portraits.

"I wonder how Freddy's team is doing," Jason said.

"Don't worry about them," Benny said. "Just think about doing the best we can."

CHAPTER 8

Smashed Snowmen

At 5:30, the snow sculptors were too cold and tired to work anymore. Benny hurried inside to the dining room, where he spotted his sisters and brother at a table. He rushed over to join them. "Wait till you see our snowpeople!" he said.

Pete stomped into the dining room. He sat down at a corner table.

Henry pushed himself away from the table. "I think I'll ask him to eat with us," he said.

"He still looks pretty angry," Benny commented.

"Maybe we can cheer him up. He seemed so unhappy at lunch," Jessie said.

Henry went over and sat down next to Pete. "We have room at our table," he said.

"So?" Pete snapped.

Henry shrugged. "We thought you might like to eat with us."

Pete rolled his eyes. "You thought wrong."

Henry stood up. "Well, if you change your mind . . ."

Violet knew Henry felt bad. When he returned to their table, she said, "Maybe he'll eat with us tomorrow."

"Where's Grandfather?" Benny asked. "I want to show him our snowpeople."

"He's eating later, with Mr. Mercer," Violet told him.

"I'd like to tell Jimmy about them, too," Benny said, looking around. "Where is he?"

"I don't think he's here yet," Jessie said.

"Freddy hasn't come in either," Henry added.

Mr. Mercer's helper filled plates with hamburgers and French fries and passed them down the table.

"My favorite!" Benny exclaimed.

Jessie laughed. "Everything's your favorite, Benny," she teased.

Pete ate fast and started out of the room.

"Looks like Pete's not staying for dessert," Henry observed.

"He's not even staying for second helpings," Benny put in.

Shortly after Pete left, Freddy appeared. She went from table to table asking, "Has anyone seen my glove?"

When she asked the Aldens, Benny said, "They're in your pocket."

Freddy yanked out an orange, green, and yellow glove. "The other one," she explained. "I lost it somewhere."

Jessie remembered seeing her with both gloves at lunch. "Maybe one fell on the floor," she said.

They looked all around. Benny looked under the table. No glove.

"Good thing I have another pair," Freddy said.

She stuffed the glove back into her pocket. Something fell to the floor. Freddy scooped it up quickly, but the Aldens saw it.

It was a key, with a tag attached to it.

Freddy hurried away without looking at the Aldens.

Behind the Aldens, someone asked, "What was all that about?"

It was Jimmy.

"Freddy lost a glove," Violet told him.

He shrugged. "It'll turn up."

"And she had a key," Violet said. "I wonder if it's the one Mr. Mercer's missing."

Jimmy shook his head. "Probably her room key."

"She picked it up so fast," Jessie said. "Like she didn't want anyone to see it."

Jimmy waved that away. "Freddy does everything fast," he said.

Benny told him about the snow sculpture. "Will you come and see it after supper?" he asked.

"I won't have time," Jimmy said. "I have to call my parents and take care of some things for tomorrow. I'll see it in the morning."

"Okay," Benny said. "By then we'll have even more work finished."

He didn't sound disappointed, but the other Aldens knew he was.

"Can *we* see your masterpiece?" Henry asked.

Benny brightened. "Let's go!"

Jessie laughed. "Aren't you forgetting something, Benny?"

Benny was puzzled.

"Dessert!" Jessie, Violet, and Henry said all together.

Benny glanced around. People were still eating their hamburgers.

"We'll be back in time," he assured them.

They trooped out of the dining room and into the lounge, where Watch was lying by the fire. He joined the parade. Benny led them all outside, down the stairs, and across the lawn. It was dark, but floodlights poured bright pools onto the snow.

Nearly running now, Benny said, "It's around the side." When he turned the cor-

ner, he saw a long shadow disappearing behind the lodge.

Watch began to bark.

"Quiet, boy," Jessie directed. "Everything's all right."

But as she and Henry and Violet came up
beside Benny, Jessie knew she had spoken
too soon.

Chunks of snow were scattered everywhere. Two of the forms were completely
bare. Pieces of wood and bits of pipe stuck
out from the other snowpeople like broken
bones.

Watch ran around, sniffing and barking.

"Our snowpeople!" Benny said, stunned.
"What happened?"

No one had an answer.

CHAPTER 9

Tracks

The Aldens stood close together, silently looking at the fallen snow figures.

Henry put an arm around Benny's shoulder. "Maybe it was an accident," he said, hoping to comfort his brother.

Benny didn't respond.

"What kind of accident?" Violet asked.

Henry shrugged. "Not an accident exactly," he answered. "What I mean is, maybe an animal did it. A raccoon or something."

Benny shook his head. "A person did it,"

he said angrily. "On purpose. I just know it."

Jessie saw something on the path beside the snow sculptures. She squatted down for a better look. "Benny's right," she said. "Look at these."

"They're tracks," Violet said.

"*Boot* tracks," Henry added.

Benny knelt down on the snow. "Pete's boots," he said.

"How can you tell?" Henry asked.

"Look at the pattern," Benny said. "It's the same as the one Pete's boots made in the dining room at lunch."

Violet searched her memory. Pete's large orange boots did leave a pattern of snow on the wood floor. "Stars," she remembered.

Henry examined the print. The star shapes were barely visible outlines on the surface of the snow. Other shapes stood out more. It was the reverse of the pattern on the floor.

"The stars on the boot must be indented — sort of like cookie cutters," he said.

"So the snow packs into them and drops out later," Jessie concluded.

"Pete did it," Benny said.

"You can't be sure, Benny," Violet said. "There could be other people with boots like that."

"He left the dining room early, didn't he?" Benny argued. "And I saw him out here."

Henry was surprised. "You saw him?"

Jessie asked, "When?" and Violet, "Where?"

Benny pointed toward the back of the lodge. "He was just going around that corner when we came out here."

"You're sure it was Pete?" Henry asked. "It's pretty dark out here. Could it have been someone else?"

Benny shook his head. "It was Pete's shadow," he said.

"Pete's shadow?" Violet repeated.

"If it was only a shadow, Benny, you can't be sure it was Pete," Jessie said.

"Let's go back to the lodge, and think this through," Henry suggested.

"I'm too upset to think," Benny said.

"Are you too upset to have dessert?" Violet asked.

Benny sighed. "I suppose I could eat a little."

Henry chuckled. "That's our Benny," he said.

Benny found his teammates Jason, Alan, and Debbie in the lounge. He told them what had happened, but he didn't mention Pete. They raced outside to see for themselves.

Pete was not in the lounge or the dining room.

"He's probably hiding," Benny decided.

The Aldens picked up their dessert plates from the front table and sat down to eat. Watch lay down at Jessie's feet.

"Why would Pete do such a thing?" Henry wondered aloud.

"He's angry because he has to be time-keeper," Violet said.

"But he's on *Freddy's* team," Jessie reminded them. "Wouldn't he want to get back at her?"

"Maybe he ruined their snow sculptures, too," Benny put in.

That was possible. They decided to check.

"But first," Benny suggested, "we should all have a second piece of pie."

Jason, Alan, and Debbie came rushing up to the Aldens' table.

"We know who did it!" Jason told Benny.

Benny looked up at him. "So do I," he said.

"That dog of yours," Jason said.

The Aldens looked at each other in disbelief.

"Watch did it all right," Debbie said.

"What makes you think that?" Henry asked.

"The tracks," Alan said.

"We saw dog tracks," Debbie added.

"It had to be Watch," Jason concluded. "He's the only dog here."

Watch lowered his head and scooted under the table.

CHAPTER 10

Another Clue

Watch destroying the snow-people? The idea made Henry laugh.

"Watch wouldn't do that," he said.

Benny was angry. "He *didn't* do it," he said. "He was in the lounge the whole time." Benny reached under the table and patted Watch's head.

"Then how'd the tracks get there?" Jason challenged.

"We took Watch with us when we went out to see your snow sculpture," Violet explained.

"He went wild," Jessie added. "He ran around sniffing and barking. He knew something was wrong."

"If Watch didn't do it, who did?" Debbie asked.

"I'll bet Watch knows," Benny said.

"That's silly," Jason said.

"He's right," defended Violet. "Dogs' noses are sensitive. Watch must have picked up the scent. He knows who did it."

"A lot of good that does us," Jason said.

"Did you see any other tracks out there?" Benny asked. He wanted to know if they had seen Pete's boot prints.

"There were tracks all over the place," Alan said.

"Lots of different tracks," Jason put in.

Benny's eyes widened. The only tracks he had seen were Pete's. "Whose were they?" he asked.

Henry laughed. "They were probably ours, Benny."

"Oh, right," Benny said. "I forgot about that."

Jason sank to a chair. "What're we going

to do now?" he asked. "We don't have a chance of winning."

"The judging isn't until tomorrow afternoon," Jessie said.

"But there's so much work," Jason argued.

Debbie sighed. "At least the forms are there. They weren't destroyed."

"And we have all morning to work," Alan said.

"Why don't we meet early?" Benny suggested.

"That's a good idea," Debbie agreed.

"Before breakfast," Alan said.

"*Before* breakfast?" Benny repeated. He hadn't meant *that* early.

"It's the only way we have a chance of finishing," Alan argued.

Alan was right, they finally decided.

The Aldens took their plates to the kitchen. Then, they went to check on the other snow sculpture. Watch padded along beside them.

Freddy's snow builders had not made much progress. It was hard to tell what the sculpture would be. But it was easy

to see that no damage had been done to
it.

Benny still thought that Pete was guilty.

"But Pete's angry at *Freddy*, not Jimmy,"
Jessie said, repeating her earlier doubt.

"Maybe he's acting," Violet suggested.
"Maybe Pete is only pretending to be angry
at Freddy."

"Why would he do that?" Henry asked.

"To throw everybody off the track," Violet said.

Benny shook his head. "I don't get it."

"Suppose Pete really wants Freddy's team
to win, but he doesn't think they have a
chance," Violet explained.

"He might do anything to make sure the
team wins. Is that what you're saying, Violet?" Jessie asked.

Violet nodded. "If he acts as if he doesn't
care about his team, no one will suspect
him."

"If Pete had a plan like that, he would have
remembered to cover his footprints," Jessie
said.

"And what about the missing keys and the

flat tires?" Henry said. "I think they're all connected."

"Let's go back to Benny's snowpeople," Violet suggested. "We might see something we missed."

At the site, Watch ran this way and that, sniffing as he had before. Benny searched for Pete's boot prints, but they were gone, covered over by other tracks.

"Our evidence has disappeared," he said.

Watch stopped beside a large chunk of snow. He sniffed. He scratched.

"What is it, Watch?" Jessie asked.

The dog kept scratching at the snow. Finally, he grabbed something orange, green, and yellow in his mouth, trotted over, and dropped it at Jessie's feet.

"It's a glove!" Violet identified.

"It's *Freddy's* glove!" Jessie said.

CHAPTER 11

A Fresh Start

The Aldens trudged back to the cabin silently. Each was deep in thought. Finding the glove in the snow near the smashed sculpture was a shock. It belonged to Freddy; that much, they knew. But they weren't sure what it meant.

In the cabin, Jessie put Freddy's glove on the table. Henry made a fire. Violet and Benny changed into their flannel pajamas. Then, they all settled close to the fireplace.

Finally, Benny spoke. "Now, we have two clues."

"Pointing in different directions," Henry said.

"Pete could have put Freddy's glove in the snow to make it look like *she* did it," Violet said.

"If he did that, wouldn't he remember to cover his tracks?" Henry said. He shook his head. "I don't think he did it. His prints don't mean any more than Watch's do."

"Do you think Freddy did it?" Benny asked.

Henry shrugged. "I don't know."

"She wants to win, that's for sure," Violet said.

They had all heard Freddy's conversation with Jimmy. She thought Jimmy's team was better. "Something has to be done to even things out," they remembered her saying. Perhaps ruining the snowpeople was her way of doing just that.

"She came in late to supper," Jessie remembered.

"And she was looking for her glove," Benny added. "She could have smashed the snowpeople while we were eating."

"If I had just done that, and my glove was missing, I'd go back to look for it," Henry reasoned. "I wouldn't tell everyone I'd lost it."

Benny yawned. "We'll never figure this one out," he said.

"What we need's a good night's sleep," Jessie said.

"Yes," Violet said. "Tomorrow they're judging the snow sculptures, and then come the ski races."

"We'll make a fresh start in the morning," Henry said.

Benny awoke at dawn. He dressed quickly and quietly, then slipped four apples into his pockets and started out. Watch followed him.

"All right, boy," Benny whispered. "You can come with me."

Outside, Watch took off on the run, his short tail wagging.

"Wait up!" Benny called. He hurried along the path behind foggy bursts of his breath.

Alan, Debbie, and Jason were already

hard at work. They had repaired one snow-person and were working on another.

"What should *I* do?" Benny asked.

"You can patch Debbie's arms," Alan answered.

Benny grinned. "Her arms look fine to me," he joked.

They all laughed.

They worked well together, much faster and better than they had the day before.

When they were half finished, Benny remembered how hungry he was. "Who wants an apple?" he asked.

Everyone did. They stood back to admire their work, and munched the crisp, tart apples.

"What will we do at breakfast time?" Jason asked. "We can't leave our snow sculpture alone."

Alan nodded. "That's right. Someone might come along and wreck everything again."

"We can take turns guarding," Debbie suggested.

Benny broke off a piece of apple and gave

it to Watch. "I have a better idea," he said. "We can leave Watch here. He's a good guard dog."

That decided, they got back to work.

At breakfast, Benny asked Violet, "What did you do with Freddy's glove?"

"We brought it with us," Violet answered. "Jessie has it."

"We're going to give it back to her," Henry said.

"We won't have any evidence then," Benny objected.

"The glove doesn't really prove anything, Benny," Jessie said. "And we might be able to tell something from the way Freddy reacts when we give it back to her."

They were on their way out the lodge door when Freddy came in with members of her team. Her smile melted when she saw the Aldens.

"Oh, Benny," she said, "I just heard about what happened yesterday. I'm really sorry."

Benny didn't respond. He didn't think she was at all sorry.

Jessie pulled the glove out of her pocket. "Freddy, we found this. I think it belongs to you."

Freddy took the outstretched glove. "Great!" she said. "Thanks."

"Don't you want to know *where* we found it?" Benny asked.

Freddy shrugged. "If you want to tell me," she answered.

Benny opened his mouth to speak, but Henry spoke first. "It was in the snow," he said.

Freddy nodded. "It wasn't in here," she said. "It had to be outside somewhere."

Violet said, "We found it near — "

"I'm sorry — I've got to go," Freddy interrupted. "I just remembered we have some planning to do." She added, "Victory speeches," and then she hurried away.

CHAPTER 12

Missing Skis

By mid-morning, Benny's team had finished their work.

"We did it!" Alan said. He smiled at the finished snowpeople.

Even Jason smiled. "I never thought we'd get done."

Benny walked around the four snowpeople. "They're good, all right," he said. "But will anyone know they're supposed to be us?"

Everyone agreed he had a point. The snow statues needed something more.

Jason took off his baseball cap and set it

on top of his snow self. "How's that?" he asked.

"Perfect!" Debbie exclaimed.

"I have an extra pair of glasses in my room," Alan said. "I could use those."

Debbie didn't know what to add. Finally, she came up with an idea: skates. "I'll put them beside her," she said.

It was Benny's turn. He tried to think of something that no one but he would have. "Oh, I know," he said at last. "My pink cup. It's back at our cabin."

Alan ran off to his room for his spare glasses, and Benny went back to the cabin for the cup. With those things in place, their sculpture was complete.

Benny and Jason smoothed away their footprints. Alan and Debbie took the water buckets back to the kitchen.

They left Watch to guard their snowpeople until judging time.

Benny hurried off to find Henry. There was time for a ski lesson. Along the way, he saw Violet, working with her ice-carving team.

"How're you doing?" he asked.

Violet shook her head. "It's hard," she said. "The ice breaks so easily."

"I'm glad I was working with snow!" Benny said.

He continued on to the ski slope. He found Jimmy in the warming house, by the fire.

"Wait till you see our snowpeople," Benny told him.

Jimmy looked surprised. "You finished?"

Benny nodded. "We didn't think we'd make it," he said.

"I heard someone wrecked your sculptures," Jimmy said. "I figured we'd have to cancel your event."

"We're going to win," Benny assured him.

Jimmy got to his feet. "I hope so," he said, but he didn't sound very hopeful.

Benny shrugged and went back outside.

Henry swooped down the slope toward him. Inches from Benny, he turned his skis to the side and came to a perfect stop. Snow sprayed everywhere.

"Can you teach me that?" Benny asked eagerly.

Henry laughed. "You have to learn to start before you can learn to stop," he said.

At lunchtime, everyone was excited. They seemed to have forgotten about the smashed sculptures and the missing keys and the flat tires. The talk was about the judging.

Nan stopped at the Aldens' table. "Violet," she said, "you should see our ice carving!" It was the first time they had seen her smile in a while.

"We're having a hard time with ours," Violet told her.

"Oh, it's hard work," Nan agreed, "but it's such fun! I'm so glad you encouraged me to sign up."

Pete stomped by in his orange boots and electric-blue earmuffs.

"Pete!" Henry called, but the boy didn't hear him.

After lunch, Mr. Mercer announced the judges' names. A group of four adults would decide each event. Grandfather couldn't be a judge because he had grandchildren in every event.

"But I'll be there cheering you on," he said.

"We will too," said Violet.

Benny said, "See you later," and went outside to wait with his team for the judging.

It was a long wait, or so it seemed. Finally, the judges appeared, followed by the spectators. Each judge carried a clipboard. First they looked at Freddy's team's sculpture, which was a huge igloo.

"Wow," Benny said. "That's great."

Then they all walked over to where Benny's team had worked. The judges walked around the snow people, nodding and making notes. No one spoke.

Finally, one said, "We have all we need."

"You've done a good job," another said.

Benny couldn't stand the suspense. "But did we win?" he asked.

"We won't know until we add the scores," a judge answered.

"And you won't know until the awards dinner," another said.

Benny and his teammates groaned. All the work they had done and redone seemed like nothing. Waiting was much harder.

After the snow sculptures were judged, everyone gathered at the ski hill. The first race was about to begin. Jimmy and Freddy were giving last minute instructions. The team members would ski down the hill one by one. Each skier's time would be recorded. The results would be added together for the team's final score.

"You can do it," Freddy told her team. "You *have* to do it."

"One minute, thirty-two and one-half seconds," Pete said and held up a stopwatch. He had been practicing for his job as timekeeper by timing Freddy's speech.

The Aldens stood near Jimmy's team. Matt was not there.

"We'll have to start without him," Jimmy said.

"But he's our best skier," someone protested.

Jimmy nodded. "I know. Without him, we can't win."

"We can try our best," Henry said.

Freddy marched over. Instead of her green hat, she wore a purple headband. "Are you ready or what?" she asked impatiently.

"We're one member short," Jimmy said. "Maybe we should just forget about the race. We don't have a chance."

Just then, Matt came out of the warming house. He ran over, his hair flopping in his face. "My skis are missing!" he announced.

Benny shot Jessie a glance. "Someone took his skis!"

"I left them over there right before breakfast," Matt said. He pointed to a rack near the warming house.

"Did you check the equipment shop?" Jimmy asked. "Maybe someone put them back in there."

Matt shook his head. "They're not there."

"Can't you borrow another pair?" Henry asked.

Matt shrugged. "That was the only pair my size."

"Use a longer pair," Henry suggested. "They're faster."

Matt tossed the hair out of his eyes. "But

they aren't as easy to control, and there's no time to practice."

Freddy shifted from one foot to the other. "So are you going to ski?" she asked Matt.

"I'll ski last," he said. "That will give me time to keep looking." He turned and ran toward the warming house.

The other skiers grabbed onto the tow and were pulled up the hill.

"Let's go look around," Benny suggested to his sisters. "Maybe we can find out what happened to Matt's skis."

He and the girls hurried to the rack where Matt had left his skis. There were tracks everywhere.

"Everyone leaves skis here," Jessie said. "We'll never be able to tell anything from the footprints."

They searched the ground, but there was no clue of any kind.

"Maybe someone took Matt's skis by mistake," Violet said.

Jessie looked doubtful. "First snow sculptures and now this. Someone doesn't want our team to win," she said.

Then they heard Mr. Alden call, "Henry's skiing next."

Jessie, Benny, and Violet ran back to watch. Freddy was just finishing her run.

"That purple headband she's wearing doesn't go with her outfit," Jessie commented.

"It's a pretty color, though," Violet said.

High above them, Henry was poised for his run. The timekeeper raised a flag, counted to three, then lowered it. The skier was off, bombing down the hill, straight for them.

The Aldens jumped up and down excitedly. "Come on, Henry!" they shouted.

When Henry reached the bottom, he came to a stop.

"Good run," the timekeeper said.

Freddy's last racer skied well.

Matt came trudging back just in time. He was wearing a pair of skis that he'd borrowed. "They're not the right length," he said, "but they'll have to do."

He skied well after all, and the whole team cheered.

There was a break before the second race. Mr. Alden took Watch for a walk. Henry snapped off his skis and headed for the rack. Jessie, Violet, and Benny walked along beside him.

"I sure hope Matt's skis turn up," Henry said.

The next race was a slalom. The team members would have to maneuver around four poles set along the slope. If a skier wasn't used to his skis, it could be especially difficult.

"We think someone took Matt's skis to keep him from racing," Benny said.

"I wonder. There have been a lot of strange things going on," Henry said, leaning his skis against the rack. Just then, something caught his eye. "What's that over there?" he asked.

They walked over to a tall juniper. There was something hung on a lower branch. It was Freddy's green knit cap!

CHAPTER 13

Too Many Suspects

Henry picked the green knit hat off the tree branch. "It's Freddy's all right," he said.

"She took Matt's skis!" Benny exclaimed.

"She might have hid them somewhere," Jessie reasoned. "Her hat must have gotten stuck on the branch as she passed by."

"But she'd have known it had gotten stuck," Henry said. "She'd feel it."

"Not if she was in a hurry," Violet argued.

Benny nodded. "She was probably scared someone would see her."

"Remember, we also found her glove near the snow sculptures," Henry said.

"But she didn't act at all guilty when we gave it back to her," Violet said.

That was true. And confusing. They had expected more of a reaction.

"She didn't even want to know where we found the glove," Jessie said.

"That's because she knew where we found it," Benny said.

A whistle sounded. The slalom race was about to begin.

Henry stuffed the cap in his pocket. "It'll take a lot more than a glove and a hat to figure out this mystery," he said. He snapped on his skis and glided toward the hill.

It was Freddy's turn, but Pete wasn't ready to clock her. His earmuffs were missing. "I put them right here on the bench," he complained loudly.

Someone volunteered to look for them while he did his job. Finally, he flagged Freddy and started the stopwatch. Her team skied very well.

"Do you suppose someone took Pete's ear-

muffs?" Benny wondered aloud.

"There are certainly a lot of things missing lately," Jessie said.

"Look," Violet said. "Our team is skiing now."

Jimmy didn't do very well. He skipped one pole and knocked over another. He left the ski hill after his run. Matt cleared the poles, but he was slow. Henry made up for lost points.

The Aldens started for the lodge.

Freddy caught up with them. "Is that my hat sticking out of your pocket?" she asked Henry.

Henry pulled it out and handed it to her.

Saying, "Thanks," she took off the headband and put on the hat. "Where'd you find it?" she asked.

As Henry was about to answer her, Jimmy approached from the opposite direction. He was carrying a pail.

"Where are you going with that?" Freddy called.

Jimmy dropped the pail into the snow. "I'm returning it to the kitchen," he said.

"Someone left it out by our snow sculpture."

Benny was surprised. "I thought Alan and Debbie took our buckets back," he said.

Jimmy shrugged. "They must've forgotten one. Unless someone else left it there . . ."

With so much going on this morning, that was certainly possible.

"What happened, Jimmy?" Freddy asked. "You blew the slalom."

Jimmy's cheeks reddened. "I know. I was really mad at myself. I guess I was worried about Matt — how he would do."

"That's too bad," Freddy said. "But good for my team. Look, they found my hat. Every time I lose something, the Aldens find it. Pretty suspicious if you ask me." Her tone was light and her eyes twinkled.

It made Benny mad. She was the guilty one. How could she accuse them of anything?

Freddy leaned over and picked up the bucket. "Come on, Jimmy," she said, "I'll walk you to the kitchen. We've hardly had any time to talk."

As soon as they were gone, Benny said,

"How could she accuse us that way?"

"She was only joking, Benny," Violet said.

"She has a point, though," Henry said. "If she isn't guilty, it must look strange to her. First we find her glove, and then I'm walking around with her hat in my pocket."

"She's guilty all right," Benny said.

"Watch didn't destroy your snow sculptures," Jessie reminded him. "But your friends thought he did."

"And for a while you were sure Pete did it," Henry said.

Violet sighed. The more she thought about this puzzle the more confusing it became. "Is there anything we can be sure of?" she asked.

"I'm sure of one thing," Benny answered. "I can't think another thought until I have something to eat."

CHAPTER 14

More Mischief

Inside the lodge, the Aldens got cups of hot chocolate and cinnamon buns and sat down by the fire.

Grandfather and Mr. Mercer came in.

"Congratulations, Henry," Mr. Mercer said. "You skied well."

"Thank you," Henry said.

"And, Benny, your snow sculpture is something to see."

Benny smiled, but Grandfather could tell something was troubling him.

"What's wrong, Benny?" Grandfather asked.

"Someone's trying to keep our team from winning," Benny blurted.

Mr. Mercer's dark eyes narrowed. "Is that so?"

"It looks that way," Henry said.

Mr. Alden sank into a chair. "We heard there was some trouble with the snow sculptures, but . . ." his voice trailed off.

"And someone took Matt's skis to keep him from doing his best," Benny said.

Mr. Mercer shook his head. "Jimmy said something at breakfast about missing skis. He wanted me to call off the race. I thought they'd turn up — that they were just misplaced." He paused. "Who could do such a thing?" he wondered.

"So many things have been going wrong — even the missing keys and the flat tires," Henry said.

"But they have nothing to do with your team," Mr. Alden said.

Henry nodded. "That's why this mystery is so confusing."

Just then, there was a commotion at the door. Nan and Pete were shouting at each other and tugging at something.

"Here, here. What's going on?" Mr. Mercer called.

Nan and Pete marched over. Each had hold of one of Pete's blue earmuffs. They were tugging so hard that the metal connecting band was stretched to its limit.

"She won't give me my earmuffs!" Pete complained.

"He ruined our ice carving!" Nan snapped. "We were making a castle. Now, the tower's gone." She wiped her tears with her red scarf. "Pete did it," she concluded. "We found his earmuffs right there in the snow."

Pete rolled his eyes. "I didn't do it," he defended. "Someone *took* my earmuffs."

The Aldens exchanged disbelieving glances. Now, the mischief was aimed at *both* teams.

Everyone trekked outside to look at the ice carving Freddy's team had made. The entire castle tower had melted away.

"The sun didn't do it," Mr. Mercer decided. "It doesn't work that fast."

"I didn't do it, either," Pete said.

The Aldens thought he was telling the truth. He was too busy with his stopwatch. He wouldn't have had the time to melt the ice.

"What happened?" Jimmy asked, walking up to the group clustered around the melted ice sculpture.

Nan told him.

"We have to call off this event," Jimmy said. "There isn't enough time to finish before the judging tomorrow."

Mr. Mercer shook his head. "Don't worry," he said to the ice carvers. "We'll figure out something."

"How can we make a castle without a tower?" Nan asked.

"Make something else," Benny suggested.

"We'd better go check *our* sculpture," Violet said, and they all paraded over there. Violet's team's ice carving had not been damaged.

"That's a relief," she said.

Just then, Freddy and Beth ran to join them.

"What's up?" Henry asked.

Freddy raised her hand. In it was Benny's pink cup.

"Hey," Benny said, "what're you doing with my cup?"

"I found it at the rink, Benny," Freddy told him.

Benny's mouth dropped open. The last time he had seen his cup, his snow self was holding it.

"Someone's ruined the ice," Beth said. "Patches are chipped and broken. People trying to skate there would have trouble staying on their feet. Racing or figure skating would be impossible."

Freddy held up a chisel. "Whoever did it used this."

"Who could've done this?" Benny wondered aloud.

Beth and Freddy stared at him.

"Wait a minute," Benny said. "You don't think *I* did it?"

"Of course they don't, Benny," Jessie assured him.

Freddy held up the cup again. "Whoever

left this here wanted us to think you did it," she said and gave it to him.

All of a sudden, Jimmy said, "I'll see you later. I have to talk to Mr. Mercer. Maybe he'll call off the games." He dashed away.

Watching him, Freddy said, "He is really acting weird. I don't know how many times he's said we should call off the games."

Everyone headed toward the lodge.

"He probably just wants everything to go right," Beth said.

"With his parents coming for the awards dinner and everything," Jessie put in.

Freddy looked at her in disbelief. "His parents aren't coming for dinner," she said. "They never come for anything. They just drop him here. They don't even pick him up until everyone else has gone home."

"But he told us they were coming," Benny said.

"Wishful thinking," Freddy responded.

Matt rushed up. "My skis are back," he told them. "I just found them in the equipment shop."

"This is getting stranger and stranger," Freddy commented.

After dinner, Mr. Mercer clapped for silence. "As you all know, we've had some trouble this year," he said. "First the keys to the equipment shop were missing, then my tires were flat. Someone damaged the snow sculptures and one of the ice carvings." Then, he went on, "Jimmy Phelps came to talk to me at breakfast this morning. He thought we should call off the ski race because Matt's skis were missing."

Henry leaned toward Jessie. "Didn't Matt say he left the skis by the rack just before breakfast?" he whispered.

Jessie searched her memory. "I think so," she said.

"And he didn't know they were missing until the race?"

Jessie nodded.

"How did Jimmy know they were missing *at* breakfast?"

Her eyes wide, Jessie looked at her brother. Did he think Jimmy had caused all the trouble?

CHAPTER 15

The Solution

"Now I've just learned that the ice at the rink has been ruined. But we're not going to cancel anything," Mr. Mercer said. Then he announced a new schedule. The ice-carving judging would be postponed. A crew was hosing the ice, and the skating competition would take place when it was ready. Sledding would be moved into its time slot.

"My message to whoever caused the trouble is this," Mr. Mercer concluded. "It won't work. Snow Haven Lodgers never quit!"

Everyone cheered.

Henry and Jessie were on their feet, ready to go.

"Come on," Henry urged Violet and Benny. "Let's go back to the cabin."

"But I haven't finished my cake," Benny protested.

Jessie pulled a paper napkin from the holder in the center of the table. "Wrap it in this," she said, "and bring it with you."

Grumbling, Benny did as he was told.

Henry and Jessie raced through the lounge with Violet and Benny trailing along behind.

Outside, Violet asked, "Why are we in such a hurry?"

"We have a new suspect," Henry told them.

"Not another one," Benny groaned. "There are already too many."

"But this might be the *right* one," Jessie said.

They wouldn't say another word until they were settled back at the cabin with a fire burning in the fireplace.

Then, Henry said, "So far the clues have pointed to Freddy and Pete."

"And all of us," Jessie added.

"Watch, too," Benny put in.

"We know it wasn't Watch or us," Violet said.

"It looks as if it wasn't Freddy or Pete either," Henry said.

Violet and Benny couldn't stand the suspense. "Then who was it?" they both asked.

"Violet, remember what you said?" Jessie asked. "That it might be someone we hadn't even thought about?"

Violet nodded.

"Well, you were right," Jessie said.

"It's the *last* person we would have thought," Henry added. He paused to let that sink in.

"Don't tell me it was Mr. Mercer!" Benny exclaimed.

They all laughed.

"No, no, Benny," Henry said. "Jessie and I think it was . . . Jimmy."

"Jimmy?" Benny repeated.

"But why?" Violet said.

Henry glanced at Jessie.

"Don't look at me, Henry," she said. "I

don't have the answer to that question."

"We'll leave the *why* till last," Henry decided. "Maybe it'll come to us as we answer the other questions."

"What made you think of Jimmy in the first place?" Violet wanted to know.

"He asked Mr. Mercer to cancel the ski race *at breakfast*," Henry explained, "but not even Matt knew his skis were missing until after lunch."

"The only way Jimmy could have known is if *he* took them," Violet concluded.

"What about our snowpeople?" Benny asked. "Freddy came late for supper. She had time to smash them."

"Jimmy was late, too," Jessie remembered.

"There's the ice sculpture," Violet said.

They fell silent trying to figure out when and how Jimmy could have done that.

Suddenly, Benny knew the answer. "The pail!" he said.

They looked at him curiously.

"Don't you remember? We were going for a snack and Jimmy came along carrying a pail."

"That's right," Jessie said. "He told us he'd found it by your snow sculpture, Benny."

"But Alan and Debbie brought our pails back to the kitchen," Benny said. "I'm sure of it."

"Jimmy must have carried hot water in it," Henry concluded. "He probably poured it on the ice castle to melt it."

"There's still the ice rink," Jessie reminded them.

"Everyone was too busy today to do much skating," Henry said. "Jimmy could've chopped up that ice any time."

"He left the ski hill after his turn," Benny said. "He probably did it then."

"Before he melted the castle," Jessie added.

"What about the missing keys?" Violet asked.

"And the flat tires?" Benny added.

"I'm not sure about those things," Henry said. "Jimmy did have the chance to do them, but — "

"That's right!" Benny interrupted. "Mr. Mercer said he parked the truck by the ice rink. Jimmy went skating that morning — before breakfast!"

"The keys disappeared the first day," Violet said. "Jimmy could have taken them when he signed the guest book."

They decided to take a break from thinking. Jessie got out their homemade cookies and poured juice. Benny unwrapped his cake. They ate in silence.

Finally, Violet said, "I guess we've answered all the questions."

"Except the most important one," Henry responded. "We still don't know *why* he did it."

Jessie nodded her agreement. "The only person who knows the answer to that is Jimmy."

"Well, then," Benny said, "we'll have to ask him."

CHAPTER 16

The Motive

The children agreed to talk to Jimmy privately and ask him why he had tried to ruin the games. But, the next morning, Jimmy did not show up for breakfast. And no one had seen him.

"Maybe he's in his room," Benny said.

Henry asked Freddy for Jimmy's room number.

"I don't think he's there," Freddy said. "I knocked this morning. He didn't answer."

"Do you suppose he's sick?" Violet asked.

"There's only one way to find out," Henry replied.

The Aldens headed down the long lodge hall. They stopped before Jimmy's door.

Benny's idea had sounded simple. But now that they were about to face Jimmy, they were having second thoughts.

"What'll we say?" Benny whispered.

"We'll think of something," Henry said. He took a deep breath and knocked.

No answer.

He knocked again. "Jimmy?" he called. "It's Henry Alden."

"Ask if he's sick," Violet urged her brother.

"Are you all right, Jimmy?" Henry called.

Silence.

The Aldens stood quietly for several seconds.

"Maybe we should get Mr. Mercer," Violet whispered. "If Jimmy's sick, he might need help."

They turned to leave. The door opened slowly. Jimmy peeked out. He looked pale. Even his cheeks had lost their rosy color.

"Oh, Jimmy," Jessie said. "You weren't at breakfast; we thought you might be sick."

"I — uh — just wasn't . . . hungry," Jimmy said.

"Then you *must* be sick," Benny commented.

That made everyone — even Jimmy — smile.

"We'd like to talk to you," Henry said. "About the games."

At first, Jimmy was silent. Then, he said, "Come on in."

They followed him into his room.

Henry cleared his throat. "We've been trying to figure out who's responsible for all that's happened," he began.

"We thought it might be Freddy or Pete," Jessie added.

"So their team could win," Benny said.

"But then their own ice carving was melted," Violet said.

"I did it." Jimmy's voice was so quiet the Aldens weren't certain they'd heard it.

After a brief silence, Henry said, "You did?"

Jimmy sank down on the edge of his bed. "All of it," he said.

Benny nodded. "We thought so," he said.

"You planted Freddy's glove and hat?" Henry asked.

Jimmy nodded.

"And Pete's earmuffs?" Jessie asked.

Jimmy nodded again.

"And my cup?" Benny wanted to know.

"Yes," Jimmy told him.

"That's what was so confusing," Henry said. "There were so many suspects."

"I didn't want anyone to take the blame," Jimmy explained. "First, I took the keys and let the air out of the tires. I didn't leave clues then. I thought that would be enough. Mr. Mercer would stop the games. But it didn't work."

"Why did you want the games stopped?" Jessie asked.

Jimmy sighed deeply. After a long pause, he began, "I've been coming here for years. Alone." He paused again to take a deep breath. "It was my idea to begin with. I was six or seven. I thought it'd be neat, you know, to be . . . on my own. And it was fun. I liked it a lot. But it got to be a regular thing. Every year, my parents would drop me here and go to some other place." He rarely saw his parents, Jimmy told them. Mr. and Mrs. Phelps were busy lawyers. Now Jimmy wanted to spend vacation with them. If the Snow Haven winter games were canceled, maybe they'd start taking him along with them.

"Have you ever told them how you feel?" Violet asked softly.

"No," Jimmy admitted. "They're my parents; they should *know* how I feel."

"They're not mind readers," Henry said.

"Even if I did tell them, they wouldn't care," Jimmy argued.

Benny sat down beside Jimmy. "That's what we thought about our grandfather," he said.

Jimmy looked surprised. "Mr. Alden is a terrific man."

"But we didn't know that at first," Violet said.

Henry told Jimmy about their days in the

boxcar and their fear of a grandfather they
didn't even know.

"We learned our lesson," Jessie said.
"Now, we say what's on our minds."

Jimmy smiled. "Benny didn't need that
lesson," he teased. "I bet he was born saying
what was on his mind."

Everybody laughed.

Then, Jimmy grew serious again. "Maybe
you're right. Maybe it's not all their fault.
Maybe it's mine, too." He looked at the Aldens. "But what can I do about it?"

They all thought about that.

Finally, Jessie said, "Why don't you call
them?"

"That's a good idea," Henry agreed.

"You mean *now*?" Jimmy sounded uncertain.

"The sooner the better," Jessie said.

Jimmy got to his feet. "All right," he said.
"I'll do it. But first, will you come with me
to talk to Mr. Mercer?"

The Aldens understood. It would be difficult to tell Mr. Mercer what he had done;
he needed support.

CHAPTER 17

The Winners

Mr. Mercer took them into his small office. There, Jimmy gave Mr. Mercer the equipment shop keys. Then, he told his story. The man sat silently, listening.

"It was a dumb thing to do," Jimmy concluded. "And I'm really sorry. I'll do anything I can to make up for it."

Mr. Mercer nodded. For a long time, he didn't say a word. He just kept nodding. The room was so quiet Jimmy and the Aldens could hear themselves breathing.

Finally, Mr. Mercer said, "Telling me this has not been easy." He paused. "I think we'll just keep it to ourselves." He glanced at Jimmy. "Is that all right with you?"

"Oh, yes, sir," Jimmy replied. The color came back to his cheeks.

"Fine. Now go on out of here, all of you." Mr. Mercer turned his chair toward his desk. "I have work to do."

They started out.

"Oh, Jimmy, there is one thing you can do," Mr. Mercer said.

"Anything, sir," Jimmy responded.

"For the remainder of the games, I expect you to do your best — like the champion you are."

Jimmy smiled broadly. "You can count on it," he said.

He went back to his room to phone his parents. The Aldens waited for him in the lounge.

"Maybe Jimmy's parents will change their minds and come for the awards dinner," Jessie said.

"I hope so," Violet said.

Jimmy came toward them. His eyes were sad.

Benny was surprised to see him back so soon. "You didn't talk very long," he said.

"I didn't talk at all," Jimmy replied. "They weren't there."

"Maybe they're out to breakfast," Violet said.

Jimmy shook his head. "They've checked out of the hotel. No one knows where they went."

At last it was time for the judging of the ice carvings. Watch sat very still beside his ice self.

"He wants everyone to know he posed for it," Benny said.

Nan's group had turned their ice castle into a dog house. Watch's name was carved on the door.

The judges called it a tie.

The next two days were busy.

As he had promised, Jimmy did his best in the remaining events. Everyone else did well, too.

Everything was more fun. The lounge was always full of people playing word games and talking. The teams mixed more freely. Benny did very well in his sledding race, and afterwards, everyone — even the adults — had a gigantic snowball fight. No one won. But it didn't seem to matter.

Skating was the last event. It was held on the afternoon of the awards dinner. Once more, the ice was smooth as glass. Beth and Jessie did figure skating dances. Jimmy and Matt raced against Freddy and another member of her team. All the skaters took part in the last race, a relay.

The crowd roared as the baton was passed from one person to the next. It was the closest, most exciting race of the week. Only Pete and his stopwatch seemed to know who had won. And he wasn't telling.

Back at the lodge, people talked about the games.

Jimmy stood by the fire, talking with the Aldens. "This was probably the best — " He broke off. The smile froze on his face.

"What's the matter?" Henry asked.

Jimmy didn't say a word. He just kept staring.

The Aldens followed his gaze. Standing inside the door were Mr. and Mrs. Phelps!

Jimmy sprang into action. "Mom! Dad!" he called and sprinted across the room to meet them.

Mrs. Phelps hugged her son. Mr. Phelps hugged him, too.

"I called you," Jimmy told them. "You'd checked out."

"We decided to surprise you," Mr. Phelps said.

Jimmy took them over by the fire. "These are my friends," he said and introduced the Aldens.

"No wonder you like it here, Jimmy," Mr. Phelps said. "There are so many interesting people."

"The whole time we were away, we kept wishing we were here with you," Mrs. Phelps said.

Jimmy couldn't hide his surprise. "And I was wishing I was there with you," he told them. After that, all his feelings came tumbling out.

The Phelps were stunned. They had always thought he wanted to come here for the winter games. And they thought he liked being on his own.

"What a terrible misunderstanding!" Mrs. Phelps said.

"From now on, we'll discuss these things," Mr. Phelps said. "And the next time we take a vacation, it will be together."

Mrs. Phelps glanced around the room. She seemed to like what she saw. "And maybe we'll spend it at Snow Haven," she said.

"That'd be great," Benny put in. "We might be here, too."

The parade into the dining room began. Mr. Alden stood at the door beside Mr. Mercer.

"Well, Benny, are you ready to eat?" Mr. Alden asked.

"I'm too excited to eat," Benny said. "I can't wait until we find out who won."

Mr. Mercer laughed. "I'll save you the suspense, Benny," he said. "In my book, you're all winners."

THE MYSTERY ON BLIZZARD MOUNTAIN

created by
GERTRUDE CHANDLER WARNER

Illustrated by Hodges Soileau

ALBERT WHITMAN & Company
Chicago, Illinois

The Mystery on Blizzard Mountain
created by Gertrude Chandler Warner;
illustrated by Hodges Soileau.

ISBN 10: 0-8075-5494-4
ISBN 13: 978-0-8075-5494-4

For more information about Albert Whitman & Company,
please visit our web site at www.albertwhitman.com.

Contents

CHAPTER 1

A Mountain of Surprise

"Left. No! No, turn right," said fourteen-year-old Henry Alden. He held the map up and frowned. "Yes, that's it. We're supposed to turn right at the next stop sign."

James Alden nodded. He was Henry's grandfather, and he was driving his four grandchildren — Henry, Jessie, Violet, and Benny — to visit the daughter of an old friend. Her name was Maris Greyson and she was a park ranger at Seven Mountains Wilderness Park.

"Are we lost?" Violet, who was ten years old, asked in a worried voice. "We've been driving for a long, *long* time."

"We're not lost," Henry said cheerfully. "We'll be there soon."

Six-year-old Benny, who had been looking out the window, said, "We haven't passed any houses for miles and miles."

"Oh — but look," twelve-year-old Jessie said. "There's a sign that says 'Greyson.' "

Grandfather turned down a very narrow, very bumpy dirt road. They rocked from one rut in the road to another.

Finally, Grandfather stopped the car in a small clearing. In the middle of the clearing was a small log cabin. The door opened and a big, furry dog came bounding out.

A woman followed the dog out into the clearing. "Shoe," she said, "heel!" The woman was small and strong-looking, with short jet-black hair. She wore jeans, hiking boots, and a red-and-black-checked wool shirt.

Grandfather got out of the car. "Maris

Greyson, it's good to see you," he said. "It's been much too long."

"It has," she said with a quick smile. "But you haven't changed." She gave Grandfather Alden a hug. "It's so good to see you, James. Welcome to Seven Mountains Park."

"Is your dog nice?" Benny asked, almost tumbling out of the car. "We have a dog, but we didn't bring him. We found him when we were living in the boxcar. His name is Watch and he's a good watchdog."

"Whoa, Benny. Slow down," said Henry. He put his hand on his brother's shoulder.

"My dog's name is Snowshoe, Shoe for short, and she's friendly to people," Maris said.

"May we pet her?" Violet asked.

"Sure," said Maris. "Shoe, come!"

"Hey there, Shoe," said Henry, bending to stroke the dog's back. "She looks almost like a wolf."

"Husky, mostly, with a few other things thrown in," said Maris. "I found her wandering on one of the trails when she was still practically a puppy. She was a skinny little thing. You wouldn't know that now, would you, Shoe?"

The dog's ears flattened when she heard her name and she wagged her tail harder.

"These are my grandchildren," said Grandfather. "Henry, Jessie, Violet, and Benny."

"Pleased to meet you. Come on in," said Maris. "I'm making stew for dinner. I'll show you where to put your gear. By the time you unpack, it'll be time to eat."

"Henry and I can unload the car," Jessie volunteered. Jessie liked to take charge and organize things.

In a few minutes, Henry and Benny were climbing up a ladder to a sleeping loft at one end of the cabin, pulling their packs and suitcases behind them.

"Wow," said Henry. "This is cool." He looked around the loft, tucked under one end of the sloping roof. Two narrow beds were pushed against each wall. A skylight let in the last rays of the sun above them.

"I like it here," Benny said. He began to unpack.

"Me, too," agreed Henry, doing the same.

At the other end of the cabin, Violet and Jessie were unpacking in a loft that looked just like the boys'. Down below, they could hear Maris talking to Grandfather as he unpacked his things. The good smell of stew filled the cabin.

"I'm hungry," Benny said suddenly. He leaned over the railing that enclosed the loft and sniffed. "Very hungry."

"Me, too," called Jessie from the other loft.

"Come on down," Maris said, looking up at them. "As soon as the table is set, we can eat."

Benny scrambled down the ladder in a flash and soon all four Alden children had the table set.

They ate hungrily. Soon they'd cleaned their plates and started on second helpings. The mountain air had made them all hungry.

"I like this cabin," said Jessie. "It's sort of like living in the boxcar."

The Aldens told Maris the story of how they had become orphans and gone to live in an abandoned boxcar in the woods. They hadn't known that their grandfather was looking for them and wanted them to come live with him.

"Then he found us and we live in Greenfield now," Violet said. "Grandfather put the boxcar in the backyard and we can visit it whenever we want."

"An amazing story," said Maris. "And now I know what to do if I ever need more room in my cabin. I'll just get a boxcar!"

Benny suddenly yawned. He covered his mouth. "Excuse me," he said.

"We should all go to bed early tonight," Grandfather said.

"I'm not sleepy," Benny insisted. But his eyes drooped.

"Going to bed early is a good idea," said Maris. "Because when you get up in the morning, I'm going to have a surprise for you."

Benny sat up. His drooping eyelids opened wide. "What is it?" he asked. "Is it a mystery? We're good at solving mysteries."

"There *are* a few mysteries in these mountains, but that's not the surprise," said Maris.

"What kind of mysteries?" asked Henry. He and the others forgot about the surprise for a minute.

"Well, the most famous mystery is the mystery of Stagecoach George," Maris said.

"Who is Stagecoach George?" asked Jessie.

"Once upon a time, about a hundred years ago, or maybe more, a very unlucky bandit named Stagecoach George robbed the local stagecoach. It was carrying a big strongbox full of gold to the bank. He got the loot, made his escape, and headed for what is now Blizzard Gap. He knew no one could catch him in these wild mountains.

"But Stagecoach George never had any luck that wasn't bad," Maris went on. "He got halfway up Blizzard Mountain — that's the tallest and wildest of these mountains — and the snow started falling. His horse was getting tired, too. So George decided to bury the loot and come back for it later.

"He'd just finished hiding the loot when his horse went crazy on him. The horse snorted and reared and then it jerked the reins free from George's hand and tore off down the mountain."

"Oh, no," breathed softhearted Violet. "Poor Stagecoach George!"

"That's when he heard an awful roar up the mountain above him, like a thousand trains thundering down the track with a thousand tornadoes right behind them."

"Uh-oh," Benny said. "I bet I know what that was!"

"Right," Maris said. "And George knew just what it was, too. It was an avalanche. He jumped just like his horse had done — for it had known something was wrong, the way animals do. Anyway, George jumped and tried to run, but it was too late."

"And that was the end of Stagecoach George?" asked Henry.

"Yep," Maris said. She leaned back. "Except some people claim they've seen his ghost. They say it's guarding his treasure, trying to figure out a way to dig it up and take it off the mountain."

"Wow," said Jessie. "That's a great story. Maybe we can find the treasure!"

"Or the ghost," said Benny.

"No such thing as a ghost," Grandfather reminded them. "But it *is* a good story."

"And there might be such a thing as treasure buried by the avalanche," Maris said. She shook her head. "At least, some people still think so."

"Can we go look for the treasure on Blizzard Mountain?" Benny asked.

"Hmmm. We *might* be able to arrange a trip to the mountain," Maris said. "Now who wants dessert?"

"Just a little," said Benny.

Everyone laughed and Benny grinned. He never said no to dessert.

Benny went to bed with his head full of stagecoach robbers and surprises. He was sure he would never be able to fall asleep.

But the minute he closed his eyes, he fell into such a deep sleep that he didn't even notice his brother climbing up into the loft or hear Henry say softly, "Night, Benny," before he, too, got into bed and fell asleep.

Jessie fell asleep right away, too. But Violet lay awake for a little while longer. She thought about stagecoach robbers and avalanches and ghosts. Once, she thought she heard a sound outside the cabin. She peered through the narrow window by her bed, but she couldn't see anything except how very, very dark it was.

CHAPTER 2

Lost Treasure

"What's the surprise?" Benny demanded first thing the next morning.

Maris slid a plate of pancakes in front of Benny and said, "It's a camping trip."

"A camping trip! I like camping," said Benny.

"I need to do a little trail scouting on Blizzard Mountain for a couple of days and I wondered if you would like to come along," Maris said.

"Blizzard Mountain? That's where the treasure is!" Benny cried.

"Yes!" said Jessie. "We'd love to come along!"

But Violet had a question. "What's trail scouting?" she asked.

"Well, here in Seven Mountains Park, we try to close trails that are getting worn out by too many hikers and climbers," Maris explained. "They're not as safe, and it's hard on the land around the trails, too. So we give the trails and the land a rest, and work on rebuilding the trails and making them safe again."

"That's a good idea," said Henry.

Maris nodded and smiled and went on, "We're closing the Annie Oakley Trail on the east side of Giant Mountain at the end of this season, and we're going to open a new trail on Blizzard Mountain. Part of my job is to hike Blizzard Mountain and mark the best way for the trail to go. We've already started work on it, but we have lots more work to do."

"Trailblazing," said Henry. "We'll be trail-blazers."

"Let's go," said Benny. "I'm done with breakfast."

Maris laughed. "Not so fast, Benny," she said. "We've got a few things we need to do first to get ready. We need to pack. And we'll have to stop in Blizzard Gap to get some gear and supplies," Maris said.

"Are you coming with us, Grandfather?" asked Violet.

But Grandfather shook his head. "No. I'll stay here with Shoe. We can do a little hiking around the cabin."

"Wouldn't you rather be an explorer?" Benny asked.

"You go explore, Benny," Grandfather said. He laughed. "Who knows? Maybe you'll even find the treasure."

"Yes, we will," said Benny confidently. He didn't mind when Maris laughed. He was sure that a mystery was waiting for the Aldens up on Blizzard Mountain.

A little while later, Henry had tossed the last backpack into the back of Maris's truck, on top of all the other camping gear he and Jessie had loaded. "That's the last of it," he said.

"We're ready to go, then," said Maris.

The children climbed into the truck. It was a tight fit. They waved good-bye to Grandfather and Snowshoe.

Then Maris turned the key in the ignition.

Nothing happened. She tried again. *Click, click* went the key. But the truck wouldn't start. Maris frowned. "What is wrong with this truck? I just did some work on it." She got out and opened the hood of the truck and peered inside. Grandfather came to join her.

"Oh, no. It might be the battery," Maris said. She got back in the truck again and turned the key. Still nothing.

"You're right, Maris," Grandfather said. "It must be the battery."

With a sigh, Maris got out of the truck. "That's the second time in two weeks!" she said. She put her hands on her hips and frowned at the battered red pickup truck. "I don't believe this! I'll go call Carola Gallo for help. She's my closest neighbor."

Soon an old blue van came bouncing down the dirt road that led to Maris's cabin.

A tall woman with a wiry build and thick blond and gray hair got out.

"Thanks for coming," Maris said. "Sorry to call so early."

"I'm always up early," Carola said crisply. "And I have an appointment over in the county seat today anyway. You're right on the way."

Maris introduced all the Aldens. Carola gave them a quick nod. She said to Maris, "Battery again? Maybe it's time for a new truck."

"Ha," said Maris. Carola got some jumper cables and attached them to her truck's battery and the battery of Maris's truck.

Maris got in her red truck and turned the key. Her truck started.

"It's fixed! Now we can go to Blizzard Mountain!" said Benny.

"Blizzard Mountain?" Carola asked.

"We're going to help Maris start work on a new trail," Jessie explained.

"I told you, remember?" Maris reminded her.

Carola raised her eyebrows. "So soon after those bear sightings, Maris? Do you think that's safe?" she asked.

"Carola, you're the only person who's reported bear sightings," Maris reminded her. "And we all know you don't want any people on Blizzard Mountain."

"No people? Why not?" Henry asked.

Carola shook her head, frowning fiercely. "That's not true! I just think we need to limit the number of people who use it every year. That protects the animals and where they live. Too many people tear up a park. In fact, too many people make it more like, well, a city."

"Every time we open a new trail, it's only because we've closed another one. You know that," Maris said.

"We should be closing more trails and *not* opening new trails at all. There are too many trails as it is," Carola argued.

Maris started to speak, but Carola kept talking. "If people want to go off the trails, they can hire guides to show them the way. Guides will make sure that they take care of the forest. And that they don't get lost!"

"If we put a real trail on Blizzard Mountain, at least we won't have to rescue lost hikers up there so much," said Maris with a smile.

"Hmmph," said Carola. "If you're hiking on Blizzard Mountain, I'd watch out for bears."

Carola climbed back into her van, slammed the door, leaned out the window, and added, "And just for the record — I'm more worried about the bears than I am about you." She drove away in a cloud of dust.

"Wow," said Benny. "I don't think she likes us."

"She's got a quick temper," Maris admitted. "And she loves these mountains more than she likes most people."

"Did she really see bears on Blizzard Mountain?" asked Violet.

"If she did, she's the only one. The bears avoid the people around here. If you see a bear, it's usually because it didn't see you first and have a chance to run away," Maris said. "I know I haven't seen any fresh sign of a bear near the trail. No tree markings."

"Tree markings? What are those?" asked Benny.

"Those are places where bears sharpened their claws or pulled dead trees and logs apart looking for insects. Insects and berries are a big part of a bear's diet," Maris told him.

"Insects. Yuck," said Violet, wrinkling her nose.

"It's funny that Carola forgot I was headed up to Blizzard Mountain today," Maris said. "We talked about it just a couple of days ago, when she reported the bear sightings. Oh, well, let's get started."

Once more, the Aldens and Maris piled into the truck.

"Is Blizzard Gap far?" asked Benny as they drove away.

"Not too far," Maris answered. "But we have to make another stop first."

"Where?" Violet wanted to know.

"To get Bobcat," Maris said.

"A bobcat!" Violet gasped.

CHAPTER 3

No Such Thing as Ghosts

"Not a real bobcat, Violet," Maris reassured her. "Bobcat. Bob Leeds. Everyone calls him Bobcat. He's a park ranger and an expert on bobcats, too. That's why he's called Bobcat," Maris said.

She turned down a long, bumpy road, which led to a stone house not much bigger than Maris's cabin. A round man with round glasses came out. He waved, closed the door of his cabin, and lifted a large backpack from the porch. He walked to the back of Maris's truck and tossed the pack in.

Then he came around to join the Aldens and Maris.

"Hi there. I heard you were coming," said Bobcat with a grin.

"I like your hat," Jessie said. It had a paw-print design on the front. "Is that a bobcat track on it?"

"Yep," he said. "Not actual size, of course."

"How big is a bobcat?" asked Violet.

"Oh, the average is about the size of a medium-to-small dog," he told them.

"And they don't eat people?" Violet asked, just to make sure.

"Nope. Too small. They're also very shy. My job is to gather more information on them so we'll be able to do a better job of protecting them."

"Protecting them? From bears?" asked Benny.

"People, mostly," Bobcat answered.

"Don't you want trails in the park, either?" asked Jessie. "Are you like Carola?"

"I agree with Carola and I disagree with her," Bobcat said. "The park belongs to everybody, but that means that everybody has to help take care of it, too. Part of taking care of it is staying on the trails and not tramping through important habitat."

"What's a habit . . . habit . . . ?" Benny asked. He'd never heard that word before.

"Habitat," Bobcat repeated. "All it means is home. Where the animals live. You could say that your hometown is your habitat, Benny. And I guess you wouldn't much like it if someone took a walk right through your front door."

"No way!" said Benny.

"Well, neither would a bobcat. So part of my job is to make sure park trails don't go through a bobcat's front door, either."

Just then, Maris slowed the truck down. "Blizzard Gap," she announced. "This is Main Street."

Blizzard Gap was much smaller than Greenfield. Maris drove by a gas station with a sign that said LULU'S GAS 'N' GO, a building with a general store on one side and a diner on the other, and a neat white house with a post office sign out front.

Above the general store, a sign advertised
GROCERIES AND EVERYTHING ELSE.

Maris parked in front of the diner.

"Why don't you kids get some hot
chocolate in the diner while Bobcat and I
get some camping supplies at the general
store," Maris said.

"Okay," said Benny cheerfully. "I like hot
chocolate."

As the Aldens walked into the diner, people turned to look at them. Violet blushed
a little. She was shy.

But Benny smiled at everyone. "Hi," he
said. He even waved at a man with curly
black hair as they passed his table on the
way to the counter.

The man looked surprised. "Hello," he
said in a gruff voice. He smiled a little.
His teeth were big and white against his
beard.

A tall, thin waitress with silver hair came
over to take their order. The name embroi-
dered on her shirt said RAYANNE.

"Menu's on the wall," Rayanne said. She
nodded toward a big blackboard at the back

of the diner. "Regular items on the left, specials on the right."

"Hot chocolate, please," said Benny. The others ordered hot chocolate, too.

"And I don't suppose you would want whipped cream with it?" Rayanne asked.

"Yes! Please!" Benny said loudly.

One side of the waitress's mouth turned up a little and her eyes crinkled in amusement. "I'll see what I can do," she said.

Henry took a map out of his jacket pocket. He unfolded it and spread it on the counter so Benny, Jessie, and Violet could see it. "Here's where we are now," he said. "And here's where Maris's cabin is."

"There's Blizzard Mountain," Violet said. "That's where we're going."

"If we don't have any more bad luck today," agreed Jessie.

Henry frowned. "I sort of wonder if someone didn't make that bad luck for Maris," he said in a low voice.

"What do you mean, Henry?" asked Violet.

"Carola made it pretty clear she doesn't

want anyone building new trails. Maybe she's been fixing Maris's truck so it wouldn't start, to try to discourage her," Henry said.

"It didn't work," Violet pointed out.

"No. We're still headed for Blizzard Mountain," Jessie said.

"And she helped fix Maris's truck both times," Benny said.

Just then, Rayanne returned with their drinks.

"Blizzard Mountain?" asked Rayanne as she set the four cups of hot chocolate in front of the Aldens. "You kids headed up that old mountain?"

"Yes," said Henry.

"I hear it's a bad luck mountain," said Rayanne. "Haunted, too."

"We know all about Stagecoach George," said Jessie. "We're not afraid of ghosts."

The man with black hair spoke up from the next table. "I wasn't afraid of ghosts, either, until this happened," he said. He leaned over and thumped his leg. "It broke my ankle for me."

"Ah, Chuck, everybody knows you saw your shadow and thought it was a ghost and that's how you broke your ankle," one of the other waitresses teased.

"Ha-ha," Chuck retorted. "I know what I saw up on that mountain. I say if it looks like a ghost and sounds like a ghost, it's a ghost."

"You saw the ghost of Stagecoach George?" Benny said. He almost spilled his hot chocolate, he was so excited.

"That's right, young man," Chuck said. He flashed his teeth in another big smile. "That's what made me fall down the mountain and break my ankle."

"Stop telling tall tales, Chuck Larson," Rayanne said. "You know there's no such thing as a ghost. And you a history teacher!"

"That's how I know so much about it," Chuck said. "It's a history teacher's job to know the history of a place he's visiting. And Stagecoach George is known to haunt Blizzard Mountain."

As Chuck finished speaking, Bobcat came in and sat down next to Benny.

"Mr. Larson says he saw the ghost of Stagecoach George," Benny reported excitedly.

"I know," said Bobcat. "I was part of the group that rescued Chuck. A hiker found him and got us, and we carried him down off the mountain. Chuck told us and everybody else to stay off Blizzard Mountain because he'd seen a ghost."

Jessie turned toward Chuck Larson's table. "If you saw Stagecoach George's ghost, you must have been near the treasure, right?" she asked Chuck.

"I don't know about that," Chuck said. "I think the ghost is still looking for the treasure, not guarding it. He doesn't want anyone to find it before him, so he haunts the whole mountain. But you know what else I think?"

Rayanne rolled her eyes. "*Of course* I know what you think. You think that the avalanche swept the stagecoach gold down the mountain and it's somewhere near the bottom and the ghost is haunting the wrong place," she said.

Chuck blushed a little. "I guess I've said it all before. It's been a few months now. But I'll never forget seeing that ghost. White and misty and floating through the trees," Chuck said. "And howling. When it started to howl, that's when I tripped and broke my ankle."

Bobcat said, "You're lucky that hiker found you when he did. You could have been stuck up on the mountain for a long time."

Again Chuck's teeth flashed in a smile. "I got pretty lost. I thought I was hiking up Pam's Peak. I guess I'm not much of a woodsman."

"If it's been so long since you broke your ankle, why are you still on crutches?" Jessie asked.

"I stumbled and reinjured it, that's all," Chuck said. "But now even a busted ankle can't keep me away from these mountains. I'm doing a history project on Blizzard Gap and this park. And according to my research, it has been a bad luck mountain ever since Stagecoach George. Look at everything that's happened up there. Floods. Lost hikers. Rock slides."

"There hasn't been an avalanche in these mountains in over sixty years," Rayanne said. "And floods happen all over these parts when the spring snow melts and it rains."

"How do you know that?" asked Bobcat. "You must like these mountains better than you think, to know all that about 'em, especially since you've only been here since the summer."

Rayanne shrugged. "I'm not a big hiker, but the mountains are pretty to look at," she said.

Chuck stood up and reached for a pair of crutches propped on a chair next to him. His chair fell over with a crash. When Chuck made a grab for the chair, he overturned the sugar bowl. Packets of sugar slid across the table.

Jessie jumped up and righted the chair. Then she put the sugar packets back in the bowl.

"Thanks," said Chuck. Then he began to limp awkwardly toward the bathroom in the hall between the restaurant and the general store.

"If you ask me, he broke his ankle just being plain clumsy," said Bobcat.

"Ghosts. Bad luck. Phooey," said Maris, who'd just come in. "The only reason people still talk about that old story is because nothing ever happens in Blizzard Gap. The last big crime around here was when someone painted the doors of the firehouse blue!"

"No, it wasn't," Rayanne said suddenly.

Everyone looked at Rayanne. She said, "Remember the burglary at the Seven Mountains Museum over in the county seat?"

Maris said, "How did you know about the robbery, Rayanne? You didn't move to Blizzard Gap until after it happened."

"Heard about it," Rayanne said. "All the news in town goes through this diner and a waitress is just naturally going to hear most of it."

"Folks around here are saying it was the work of professionals," said Bobcat. "I mean, look at what the robbers took. Gold bricks. You have to plan a robbery to haul away gold bricks. They're heavy!"

"The museum didn't have much security," remarked Rayanne. "It couldn't have been such a hard place to break into. They say there was no sign of a break-in."

"Doesn't that just prove the burglars were professionals?" asked Chuck, who'd come back in and settled again at his table. "Probably a whole gang of thieves. From a big city somewhere."

"What else did the robbers take?" asked Henry.

"Nothing else except a purple velvet cape. But it was historically priceless," said Rayanne. "It was worn by Jenny Lind, a famous singer who visited the town once. She left her cape behind with the owner of the old opera house as a memento."

"Maybe that's what the robber used to escape!" said Chuck, and several people snickered. "Put on the velvet cape and flew away." Chuck flapped his arms, enjoying the audience.

Maris rolled her eyes. "Time to go," she said to the Aldens and Bobcat. They finished their hot chocolate and got up to go.

"Let's not forget the robbery wasn't actually in Blizzard Gap. It was all the way over in Millpond," Bobcat reminded everyone as they walked out of the diner.

"That's about as close as we get to crime these days," said Maris.

But then she stopped so quickly that Bobcat bumped right into her. "Oh, no!" she said. "What happened to my truck?"

CHAPTER 4

Stay Away from Blizzard Mountain!

The red pickup truck was just where they had left it. But now it was tilted to one side, like a sinking ship.

"Look," said Henry. "Both tires on one side are flat."

"Great!" fumed Maris. "This is just great!"

"It'll be okay," said Jessie. "We can fix the tires."

"Better yet, I'll get Lulu the mechanic to come over from the gas station. She can patch and pump those tires in no time flat," Bobcat said.

"Oh, okay," Maris said grumpily.

While Bobcat was gone, the Aldens all examined the tires very carefully. But they couldn't find a nail or a piece of glass or anything that would have made a hole in the tires so they would go flat.

"Someone must have let the air out of the tires," said Henry at last.

"That's what I think," Maris agreed. She folded her arms. "If I didn't know better, I'd think someone was out to get me."

"But why would anyone do that?" asked Violet.

Just then, a big white tow truck pulled up. Lulu got out of the tow truck, along with Bobcat.

"Bad luck," said Lulu, raising her eyebrows. With that, she went to work pumping air back into the tires. "No leaks," Lulu reported when she finished. "Looks like someone played a mean trick on you, Maris, and just let the air out of those tires."

Maris sighed. "Let's get going," she said.

"Or we won't even be able to start today."

"I just hope we don't have any more bad luck," said Violet in a low voice.

Jessie frowned. "Bad luck? No. I think it's more than that. A dead battery. Two flat tires."

"And all that talk about ghosts on Blizzard Mountain," said Henry. "It's almost like someone doesn't want us to go to Blizzard Mountain."

"Is it a mystery?" asked Benny eagerly.

"It might be, Benny," said Henry. "It just might be a mountain of a mystery."

Bobcat had picked up his truck at the park ranger office in town. Now he led the way in his truck, while Maris and the Aldens followed. The narrow winding mountain roads seemed to get bumpier and narrower with each passing mile. At last they came to a bare patch of dirt along one side of the road. Bobcat pulled over. So did Maris.

"Where's the trail?" Benny asked.

"Right there," Maris said, pointing.

Benny squinted and frowned. He didn't see anything but trees.

They put on their packs and reknotted their hiking boots and they each took a drink of water. Then Maris led the way toward the trees. She stepped between two trees and over a small boulder, and there it was: a faint trail threading through the trees.

Jessie could see white blazes of paint on the trees before them now, marking the trail ahead.

"It's almost like a secret trail," said Violet.

"There's been a rough trail here ever since I can remember," Maris told them. She made a face. "People using it to look for Stagecoach George's treasure, I guess."

They were passing a spooky-looking group of twisted dead trees. Jessie couldn't help asking, "Has anybody else ever seen the ghost of Stagecoach George? Besides Chuck?"

"People *say* they have," said Maris.

"Like that couple that got lost on Blizzard Mountain a couple years back," Bobcat said. "When the rescue team found them, they both said they'd seen a ghost."

"They'd been lost in the woods for three long, cold days," said Maris. "They were so scared they thought *you* were a ghost at first. Ghosts don't exist, Bobcat. Keep that in mind."

"Some of the other rangers have seen and heard strange things in these mountains," Bobcat argued stubbornly.

"But not ghosts," said Maris.

"I'd like to see a ghost," said Benny. "Then we could catch it. And if it was Stagecoach George, we could make him help us find the treasure."

Maris looked over her shoulder in surprise at Benny. "You're not afraid of ghosts?"

"No!" said Benny. "Boo to ghosts!"

Everyone laughed.

"Well, I'm glad to hear it," said Bobcat. "It's always good to have brave company in the mountains."

They walked quietly after that. Bobcat pointed out red squirrels that dashed up trees as they went by. Jessie saw a crow flapping heavily through the branches above them. Something slid into a stream with a splash when the hikers scrambled across the rocks in the streambed.

After a while, Violet said, "It's so quiet. And empty!"

"Oh, animals are everywhere around us," Bobcat said. "They can see us. Hear us, too, probably from miles away."

"I haven't seen any animals except squirrels and crows," Benny said.

"But they see you," said Bobcat. "Right now, they're sitting back and saying, 'Now, who do you suppose that is, walking right through our front yard?' "

Jessie laughed. "We'll have to be good guests and not make a mess," she said.

"Right," Maris said over her shoulder.

They hiked, stopped for lunch by another stream, then hiked some more. It got later and later.

Benny's feet began to hurt.

Suddenly Henry said, "I see a house!"

"The lean-to," said Maris. "Good. We've got just enough daylight left to set up camp." She led the way off the trail to a rough low building that looked like half of a triangle made of logs. A slanted log roof and log walls ran down to meet a log floor on the sides and in the back. The open front of the lean-to faced a stone fire pit.

"We'll camp here tonight," said Maris.

"Do we put our tent inside?" asked Benny.

Bobcat laughed. "Nope. The only things you put inside are balsam tree branches. You put those on the floor and put your sleeping bags on top. I'm going to put my tent right over there, and I'm going to put balsam tree branches in it, too."

Henry shivered. "It's getting colder," he said. "Let's build a fire right away."

"We need to hurry," Maris said. "It's getting dark."

Quickly everyone went to work. Soon the lean-to was piled with soft, sweet-smelling balsam and a fire was roaring in front of the lean-to. They sat down on the edge of the lean-to in front of the fire and made a dinner of soup mix cooked with boiling water over the fire, cheese, fruit, and bars of chocolate for dessert.

After dinner, the Aldens and Bobcat set out to explore the woods around their campsite. They had gone a little way when suddenly Jessie held out her hand. "Look! It's snowing!" she cried.

"Time to get back to the lean-to," Henry said.

They hurried back to camp. As they got closer, they saw Maris standing at the edge of the light cast by the fire. She turned a big flashlight in their direction and said, "Bobcat? Is that you?"

"It's us," said Bobcat.

"What is it?" Jessie asked. "You look worried."

"We weren't lost," Benny said.

"It wasn't that." Maris smiled. "I thought I heard something."

Everyone stopped to listen. They heard wind whispering in the trees. They saw shadows made by the fire leap up in the darkness. They felt the cold touch of snow-flakes.

But nothing more.

At last Maris said, "It must have been an animal."

"That's about the only thing that would be up here," Bobcat said.

"True," said Maris. "Okay. Let's get some rest."

Maris banked the fire so it would stay hot through the night. Then everyone got into their sleeping bags on top of the sweet-smelling balsam branches.

The night grew still. Through sleepy eyes, Benny watched the snow falling through the dim firelight.

He was almost asleep when Violet sat straight up and cried, "What's that?"

CHAPTER 5

The Hungry Thief

Everyone woke up. Maris, Henry, and Jessie switched on their flashlights.

The beams poked holes in the darkness. But nobody saw anything.

"I heard someone walking!" Violet insisted. "Over there." She pointed.

Bobcat came around the side of the lean-to from his tent. "What's going on?" he asked.

"Violet heard someone," Henry told him. He pointed.

"I'll check on the food," Bobcat said. "Maybe that's what you heard, an animal doing a little grocery shopping."

They watched Bobcat's flashlight bob away from the lean-to. A few minutes later, he came back. "Nothing," he said.

"I *know* I heard something," Violet said.

"It must have been the wind," Maris told her. "Or some small animal."

Everyone lay back down. One by one, the campers began to fall asleep.

Until Violet sat up once more. "There it is again," she cried.

This time, Maris walked to the edge of the clearing and shone her flashlight beam into the darkness all around. Everything was still and quiet. Bobcat called from his tent, "Everything okay, Maris?"

"Okay, Bobcat," she called back. To Violet, she said, "Nothing's here. Or if it is, it's run away."

"I know I heard something," Violet repeated.

Jessie put her hand on Violet's arm. "It's

just some animal," she told her sister. "The animals won't hurt us."

"It didn't sound like an animal," Violet said. "It sounded big. Like someone walking."

"A deer, maybe," said Maris, yawning.

"Or a bear?" Benny asked.

"If it was a bear, it'd make a lot more noise. It's no bear," Maris told him. "Let's get some sleep."

Everyone lay back down again. This time, it took longer for them to fall asleep. But at last, only Violet was awake. She lay with her eyes wide open, listening hard. She listened and listened.

But the woods were silent except for the creak of branches in the cold wind.

Then she heard a sound. She sat up, but she didn't say anything. She strained to hear.

The sound stopped. Violet began to relax. She lay back down. *Just a raccoon or something*, she told herself sleepily.

At last she fell asleep.

* * *

"Oh, great! That's just great!"

Bobcat was shouting. Violet sat up and blinked. A thin frosting of snow decorated everything. Tracks made patterns in the snow.

Maris stood by the warm fire heating a pan of water. "What is it, Bobcat?" Maris called.

A moment later, Bobcat came into sight. His hair was wild and he looked upset and angry.

Benny and Henry were right behind him. "It was a bear!" Benny said gleefully, before Bobcat could answer Maris.

Jessie came trotting around the other corner of the lean-to, holding her toothbrush. "Where's a bear?" she asked.

But Bobcat was shaking his head. "If it was a bear, I'll eat my hat," he said. "No bear is that neat."

"Did something eat the food?" asked Maris.

"You guessed it," Bobcat said. "About half of it is gone. Clean gone. No broken-open packets of soup, no dried noodles scattered on the ground. Just gone."

Maris frowned. "That doesn't sound like a bear."

"Did you see any footprints in the snow?" Jessie asked.

"No," said Henry. "It must have happened early in the night, when the snow had just started to fall."

"Maybe we should just give up and start over," Bobcat said.

"We have food left, don't we?" Maris asked.

"Some — " Bobcat held up a small bag of sugar. "Powdered milk. Sugar. Some dried beans. About half a dozen chocolate bars. The peanut butter sandwiches. Oh, yeah, and some dried oatmeal."

Maris made a face. "It could be worse," she said.

Jessie looked at her sister. "You were right, Violet. You did hear something!"

Maris sighed. "Well, whoever did this left us enough food for today. If we can get more supplies, we should be fine."

Now Bobcat sighed. "I'll do it," he volunteered. "I'll go back to Blizzard Gap and get more food and meet you at the next campsite."

"Can you make it all the way down and back up to the old cabin by tonight?" Maris asked.

"If I start now," Bobcat answered.

"I could come with you," Henry offered. "I can carry some of the supplies."

Bobcat shook his head. "Stay here and help with the trail," he told Henry. "I'm used to carrying a heavy backpack. It won't be a problem."

A few minutes later, as the Aldens and Maris packed up the camp, Bobcat put on his almost-empty backpack. "When you see me again," he said, "this pack will be full of groceries."

With a wave and a smile, Bobcat headed back down the trail. Soon after, the Aldens and Maris had the campsite as clean as if they'd never been there. Then they, too, put on their packs and headed in the opposite direction.

They didn't walk fast. Maris stopped to make marks on trees with paint and write notes in a small notebook. Sometimes she took photographs or drew diagrams. The snow stayed on the ground in the shade but began to melt along the trail. Their boots made wet, squishing sounds as the Aldens walked.

Maris showed them the neat, even tracks of a fox where it had crossed the trail.

"What's this?" asked Violet, pointing to another set of tracks.

"Rabbit," said Maris. "And one with a sore foot, from the looks of it."

"How can you tell?" asked Jessie.

"Look at this footprint. The other three tracks are deep. But the right front one is blurred and only deep at the toes, as if the rabbit put its foot down quickly, then lifted it up again, dragging it a little."

"Oh," said Jessie. "I see."

They hiked on. At last, when the sun was high overhead, Maris said, "It's lunchtime. Why don't you rest here? I'm going to look around and see if I can find a way

around these rocks that isn't so steep."

Benny and Jessie sat on a log. Violet found a spot on a rock in the sun. Henry spread his waterproof jacket out on a patch of leaves and sat on that. They ate peanut butter sandwiches they'd made the day before and drank water that Maris had filtered from a stream that morning. For dessert they each had a chocolate bar.

"If it wasn't a bear, I wonder who took our food last night," Henry said.

"Half our food," said Jessie. "Whoever it was left us some food so we wouldn't starve."

"A sort of nice thief," said Violet.

"Maybe it was the thief who stole all that stuff from the museum," Benny said.

"I don't think so," said Henry. "That thief would be long gone by now. But I do think it was a person, not a bear. If a bear had torn down our food bag, it would have left a big mess. There wasn't a mess. I mean, the bag had burst open, but only some of the stuff had been taken."

"The chocolate bars weren't taken," said

Jessie. "If I was a bear, I'd take *all* the chocolate bars first."

Everyone nodded. Then Violet said, thoughtfully, "It's almost as if someone were trying to scare us off, but they wanted to make sure we didn't go hungry getting back home."

"You're right," agreed Henry. "I don't think a bear would be that thoughtful."

"Then who was it?" Benny asked. He looked around. "Is someone following us?"

Violet looked around, too. She shivered a little. "I hope no one is following us, Benny," she said.

"Lots of people knew we were coming up this way," Jessie said. "Carola. Rayanne."

"Chuck," said Benny.

"All the people in the coffee shop," said Violet.

"But who would want to follow us all the way up here and steal our food?" asked Henry. "And why?"

"Not Chuck. He's got crutches," Benny said.

"Rayanne?" asked Violet.

Jessie shook her head. "I don't think so. She was busy at work."

"That leaves Carola. She doesn't want us here," said Henry.

"She could have sneaked into town and let the air out of the tires," Jessie said. "And she could have fixed Maris's car so it wouldn't start yesterday morning."

"She said she had an appointment in Millpond," Henry said.

"She could have been making that up," Jessie said. "Just like she might have been pretending not to remember Maris had told her we were hiking up Blizzard Mountain today."

"Or if she did have to go to Millpond, maybe someone's helping her," said Violet. "She fixed Maris's battery, but someone else let the air out of the tires and stole the food."

"Who?" Benny wanted to know.

They were silent for a moment. Then Henry said slowly, "It could be Bobcat."

"I like Bobcat!" Benny said indignantly.

"We all do. But he might not want people up here, either, Benny. Just like Carola," Henry said. "They could be working together."

"He was in his tent last night," said Jessie. She thought for a moment, then added, "Both times Violet heard the noise, Bobcat didn't come check on it or say anything until after the noise had stopped. So maybe he wasn't in the tent at all."

"Maybe he was being a bear," said Violet.

"It would have been easy for him to have let the air out of the tires while he was doing his errands," Henry said.

"That's right. He did other errands before he came to the diner. He could have done it then," Violet recalled.

"It wasn't Bobcat!" Benny said, sounding almost angry.

"Maybe not, Benny. I hope not," Henry said. "But — "

He didn't have a chance to say more. Maris came through the woods toward them. "Let's go," she said. "I think I've found a nice little detour around these rocks."

The Aldens jumped up and shouldered their packs. Before they left, Maris made a mark on a tree, with an arrow beneath it. "So Bobcat can find us," she said, "when he comes up the trail this afternoon."

The Aldens all looked at one another. They didn't say anything. But they were all wondering the same thing.

What if Bobcat didn't come back at all?

CHAPTER 6

A Haunted Cabin?

Late that afternoon, Violet stopped. "Look!" she said.

Through the trees, they saw an old cabin.

"That's it," Maris said. "We're here." She turned off the narrow, almost invisible path she'd been following and marking, and pushed her way through the bushes.

"Too bad old Chuck didn't know about this cabin when he broke his ankle," she said as she led the way to the cabin. "He was just down the trail. He was in his tent and snug enough. But he'd have been much more comfortable in the old cabin."

The cabin sat on a small patch of level ground, its back almost against the side of the mountain. Wooden shutters were closed tightly against the one window, but the door sagged a little and piles of leaves, branches, and straw seemed to be about to crash down on them from the roof as they got closer.

"It looks like a *haunted* cabin," said Benny.

"Not haunted. Just not used in a while. Bobcat and I did a few repairs a while back, but we haven't been here in a long time."

She pushed open the door of the cabin and led the way inside. Clouds of dust rose around her feet.

She sneezed. "Whew!" she said. "I don't remember it being this dirty when I left. It's almost like someone dumped a bucket of dirt in here."

"We can clean it up," Violet said. "Don't worry."

They dropped their packs on the rough bunk beds built along one wall. Maris put hers on the floor near the old woodstove.

Benny found a rusty basin with a bucket next to it on a shelf beneath one of the two shuttered windows. "Is this for water?" he asked.

"For washing dishes and your face," said Maris. "It's the cabin sink."

A rickety table and some stools stood near the stove. On the wall above the rusty basin was a small white metal cabinet. Beneath it, a row of tin cups hung from hooks.

"Let's get some wood for the stove," Henry said.

"Good idea," agreed Maris. "Then we can have a nice fire going to cook our food when Bobcat gets here in a little while."

But although they kept the fire hot, the sun went down and no Bobcat showed up.

"Maybe he's lost," said Benny, looking worried.

"Not Bobcat," said Maris. "He's too good a woodsman for that. He probably didn't make it down the trail in time to come back up tonight. I bet he's camped at the lean-to. He'll be here tomorrow."

No one said anything. Everyone wanted to believe that Bobcat was on his way, but none of the Aldens could be sure of that.

At last Violet said in a small voice, "What do we do about dinner?"

"Well, we've got some oatmeal, don't forget," said Maris cheerfully. "And I've got a few things in my tin cabinet over there."

She walked over to the cabinet. She peered inside. "We have a big metal canister of dried beans," she reported. "And some rice in this metal box. And I think . . . yes. Two packages of macaroni and cheese in this metal box. And a can of tomatoes! I'd forgotten about that!"

"Why is everything in metal boxes?" Benny wanted to know.

"This is my pest-proof food cabinet," Maris explained. "I lugged it all the way up here when I first laid out the trail this summer. It's metal to keep out mice, raccoons, chipmunks, and rodents. Everything inside is in metal, too, to help keep the smells inside the cabinet. That keeps any hungry bears away. If a bear can't smell anything inside, it's not going to bother."

"Wow," said Benny.

"We can make stew for dinner," Violet said. "Bean and tomato stew. With rice."

"Good idea," said Henry. He was hungry.

"Let's get to work," said Jessie.

When they had finished dinner, they settled into the bunk beds. The cabin was rough, but they were glad to be indoors. After their long hike, they had no trouble falling asleep.

They had leftover stew at lunch the next day. "And we'll have stew again tonight, too, if Bobcat doesn't get here soon," said Maris. She sounded worried.

"If Bobcat doesn't come, will we have to leave?" asked Violet.

"No," said Maris slowly. "We'll do fine on beans for another couple of days, which is how long I'd planned to be here. It's just that we're going to get mighty tired of beans."

Benny didn't say anything. He liked most

food, but he was already getting tired of beans for every meal!

After lunch, they walked farther up the mountain, helping Maris clear a section of trail. They cut back bushes and cleared away fallen trees. It was hard work.

Late in the afternoon, they returned to the cabin.

They saw no sign of Bobcat.

Maris shook her head. "If he doesn't come tomorrow, maybe I'll hike back down the trail to make sure he hasn't fallen or gotten hurt on his way up here," she said.

"What if he has?" Violet said, sounding more worried than Maris.

"Bobcat can take care of himself," Maris said. "Don't worry. He's trained in wilderness emergency rescue, just like all the park rangers are."

"Oh," said Violet.

"I'm hot," Benny announced.

"Me, too," said Jessie in surprise. "I can't believe how hot I am. Especially since it snowed the night before last."

"Hard work and sunshine," said Maris with a smile. "Why don't we head down to that stream over there and stick our feet in the water? That should cool us off."

At once the Aldens jumped up and headed for the stream. They lined their boots behind a log at the top of the little bank above the stream, then slipped and scrambled down to the water.

"It's freezing!" Violet squealed.

"It's so cold it makes my teeth hurt," said Benny, dipping one toe in and then the other.

They stood on the rocks in the warm sun and played in the water, being careful not to get anything more than their toes wet. Maris sat nearby, laughing. She splashed cold water on her face and lifted it to the sun. "This is one of the reasons I like working in this park," she said.

"I'm going to be a park ranger when I grow up," Benny said. "And a detective."

"Oh, Benny," said Violet.

They skipped stones on the water and made boats out of leaves that they sent

swirling downstream. Violet gathered a collection of pretty colored rocks from the stream.

"Look!" said Benny suddenly. "Gold!" He held out a sparkling rock. They all came to peer at it.

"I'm afraid not, Benny," said Maris. "Those sparkling chips are mica, not gold."

"It's pretty anyway," said Violet.

"Here. You can have it for your rock collection," said Benny generously.

"That's nice of you," Maris said. "And I have something you can add to your collection."

"What collection?" Benny asked, puzzled.

"Your collection of knowledge," Maris said teasingly. She bent over and showed the Aldens a small plant with waxy round leaves. It grew close to the earth. Maris broke off a leaf and rubbed it between her fingers. "Smell," she said.

Violet took a cautious sniff. "Peppermint?" she asked.

"Nooo," said Jessie.

"Gum. It smells like chewing gum," Benny said.

"It does, sort of," Henry agreed.

"You're all close. It's wintergreen," said Maris. "Just like in wintergreen gum. You can chew on it or use it to make tea out here in the woods."

"Wow," said Benny. He stuffed a leaf in his mouth and blinked in surprise at how strong the flavor was.

Maris looked at the sky. "It's getting dark. Time to get back," she said.

One by one, the Aldens scrambled up the side of the stream bank to where their hiking boots waited by the log.

And then Henry said, "Oh, no!"

"What is it, Henry?" asked Violet.

"My hiking boots!" said Henry. "They're gone!"

"Gone?" Jessie looked around. "Are you sure?"

"They were right here with everybody else's," Henry said. He pointed. "Now they're not."

"Uh-oh," said Benny. His eyes widened. "It's Stagecoach George. He's been here."

"No ghost did this," said Maris.

"Maybe it was an animal," suggested Violet.

"I guess it could be," Maris said. "But it doesn't make sense. Why would an animal take a pair of boots? *One* boot, maybe. Animals might make a meal on the leather. But a pair of boots?"

Henry said, "My feet are cold."

"Of course they are," said Maris. "Come on, Henry. Let's get back up to the cabin. You can put on a pair of wool socks. You do have extra socks, don't you?"

"I do," said Henry, looking a little more cheerful.

"We'll stay here and look around for the boots," said Jessie.

After Henry and Maris had gone, Benny, Violet, and Jessie scouted for Henry's missing boots. But they didn't find the boots, or even a clue about what had happened to them.

"I don't understand," Violet said as they walked back up to the cabin. "Do you think it's the same person who took our food?"

"It could be," Jessie said. She looked

around. "Or maybe it is an animal."

"A raccoon wearing Henry's boots," said Benny. He laughed at the idea.

Jessie smiled. But she knew that a raccoon hadn't stolen Henry's boots.

Henry stayed in the cabin the rest of the afternoon. "I'll cook dinner, since I can't hike," he said.

"I'll help," said Benny loyally.

"We'll do a little more work outside," said Maris. "And keep an eye out for Bobcat."

But once again, by suppertime no Bobcat had appeared.

No boots, either.

And their troubles were just beginning.

In the middle of the night, Violet sat up. "What was that?" she whispered.

No one answered. Everyone else was asleep.

Violet heard it again. A faint tap-tap-tapping.

Her fingers tightened on her sleeping bag. "Who's there?" she said in a louder voice.

Tap. Tap. Tap.

It was coming from outside the cabin.

Someone was tapping on the cabin wall!

Quietly, carefully, Violet leaned over and poked Jessie in the next bunk.

"Umpf," mumbled Jessie.

Violet poked her again.

"What?" said Jessie hoarsely.

"Shhh," Violet warned. "Listen."

Tap. Tap. Tap.

Now the sound was coming from across the cabin.

"Do you hear that?" Violet whispered.

"I hear it," Jessie said in a low voice.

Tap.

Tap.

Whatever it was sounded as if it was walking around the cabin.

Suddenly Benny said, "Violet?"

"Shhh," warned Violet.

Tap. Taptaptap.

The sound grew louder.

"It's the ghost!" cried Benny. "It's the ghost of Stagecoach George!"

He tumbled out of his bed and hurled

himself toward the cabin door. It was very dark, but Violet could just see Benny's shape in the dim light from the glowing stove.

"Benny, wait," hissed Jessie.

"W-what?" said Henry, waking from a deep sleep.

"What is it?" Now Maris was awake, too.

Benny didn't answer. He had his flashlight out. He threw the door open and raced into the night.

"Benny!" shouted Violet. Grabbing her own flashlight, she raced after him. Jessie was close behind.

"What's going on?" Maris said.

Violet stumbled out into the night. She saw the beam of Benny's flashlight disappear around the corner of the cabin.

She switched her own flashlight on and followed.

"Violet? Benny?" Jessie called behind her.

"This way!" Violet called back.

She rounded the side of the cabin.

"Benny!" she gasped.

But Benny had disappeared.

CHAPTER 7

Tap, Tap, Tap

"Benny!" shouted Violet.

Jessie ran up to her. "Where's Benny?" she asked.

"Help," squeaked a little voice from nearby. "Help! Help!"

"It's Benny," gasped Violet.

"Help!" Benny called again.

"Benny? Where are you?" Violet called.

"Over here!" Benny said.

They scrambled down through the bushes and tumbled out onto the Blizzard

Trail near the cabin. Benny was sitting in the middle of the trail.

"Oh, good," he said. "There you are! I was afraid you were lost."

"We weren't lost! We thought *you* were!" said Jessie indignantly.

"No," said Benny. "I dropped my flashlight and it went out. Or I might have caught the ghost."

Maris burst out of the bushes behind them and skidded to a stop. "Benny! Violet! Jessie! What on earth is going on?"

"Here's your flashlight, Benny," said Violet. She reached over and picked it up. "But I think it's broken."

"Is everybody all right?" Henry shouted from the door of the cabin. They could see him against the light from the stove inside. He was holding a flashlight, too, waving it back and forth like a searchlight.

"We're fine!" Maris called. "We're on our way back." To Benny she said, "Are you hurt?"

"Nope," said Benny. He jumped to his feet. "I almost caught the ghost!"

"Ghost! I don't want to hear it. At least, not until we get back to the cabin. Then you can tell me what happened," Maris said.

They went back to the cabin. Henry had put another log on the fire and it was warm inside. Everyone sat down, and Violet and Benny told about the tapping sound on the cabin wall.

"Tapping?" Maris repeated. "That was no ghost. It was a tree. A branch."

"I don't think it was," Jessie said.

"Me either," said Violet.

"It sounded like a person," said Benny. "Or the ghost of a person. Like this." He leaned over and tapped on the cabin wall. "Only it came from outside."

"And it moved around the cabin, like someone was circling us, tapping on the walls," said Jessie.

"And then when I ran out, I saw something run into the woods. Toward the trail. But I tripped and dropped my flashlight and everything got dark, so I stopped chasing it," Benny added.

"You saw a ghost, Benny?" asked Henry.

"Well . . . no . . ." Benny admitted. "But I did see something run into the woods."

Maris pressed her hand to her forehead. "I don't believe this," she said, almost to herself. "Why would anyone be out here in the middle of nowhere, tapping on the cabin walls?"

"I don't know, but whoever or whatever it was, I bet you all scared them away," said Henry.

"Maybe it was whoever took your boots," said Benny. He paused. "Except I don't think a ghost would come out during the day to take someone's old boots."

"No, no, no," said Maris. "Stolen boots, ghosts tapping on walls. What is going on? If I didn't know better, I'd say this mountain really was haunted."

No one spoke for a long minute. Then Jessie said, "Haunted, or maybe someone who doesn't want us here is trying to scare us away."

"But why?" said Maris.

"Carola doesn't want a trail up here," Violet reminded Maris.

"Neither does Bobcat," Jessie added.

But Maris was shaking her head. "No!" she said again. "I don't believe Bobcat would do something like this. Or Carola, either."

"Both of them knew you were coming up here," Jessie argued. "Either one of them could have flattened your truck's tires out in front of the diner."

"And both of them are skilled enough to hike around in the woods, day or night, without getting lost," Henry said. "Carola could have followed us up here and taken our food. And my boots. And tapped on the walls."

"Or maybe Bobcat never really went back down the mountain," said Violet.

Henry took a deep breath. "Or there might be another reason that someone is trying to scare us away."

"Like what?" said Maris.

"Maybe someone has found Stagecoach

George's treasure," said Henry.

To Henry's surprise, Maris suddenly laughed. "No one's ever going to find that treasure, Henry, even if it does exist. People have been looking for years," Maris said. "Enough mysteries, okay? Let's get to sleep. We've got lots of work to do in the morning."

"But — " Benny began.

"No," said Maris firmly. "Not another word about ghosts or mysteries or treasure or anything else."

So Benny kept quiet. But he knew that all the Aldens would get up extra early in the morning to look for clues.

Even though they got up at sunrise, the Boxcar Children didn't find a single clue.

"Those smudges in the mud behind the cabin here *could* be footprints," Jessie said. She sighed. "And we could have made them ourselves in the dark."

"Do you really think someone could have found the hidden treasure?" asked Violet.

"I know someone is trying to scare us

away," Henry said. "I just don't know why."

Just then someone in front of the cabin shouted, "Wake up in there, you sleepy-heads!"

The Aldens hurried toward the sound of the voice. They found Carola and Rayanne standing in the clearing.

"Carola! Rayanne!" Jessie exclaimed. "What are *you* doing here?"

CHAPTER 8

Someone's Out There!

Carola looked surprised. "Hiking," she answered. "What does it look like?"

"I thought you didn't like hiking," Violet said to Rayanne.

Rayanne struggled out of her backpack. "Did I say that?" she said. "Well, when Carola told me she was going to hike up this way, I thought I'd give it a try." She made a face. "But this new backpack I bought is a pain. And so are these shoes."

"Once they're broken in, they'll feel better," said Carola. A sudden smile creased her face. "It's the people with all the fancy new stuff that get lost up here. Someone sells them expensive new gear. Tells them it'll be sure to make them into real wilderness wonders."

"Like that history teacher who broke his leg," added Rayanne.

"Chuck," said Benny.

"Him!" said Carola. "Ha. I've never met anybody who went hiking with so much new stuff and so little experience. It's a wonder he didn't get more lost!"

Rayanne said, "Well, sounds like he learned his lesson. He keeps warning people to stay away."

"And talking about ghosts. Ha!" said Carola. "Crazy talk, if you ask me."

Maris opened the cabin door. "Carola and Rayanne! Hi," she said. "If you've got any extra coffee and are willing to share, we'll provide the hot water."

"Sure," said Carola. "Didn't you bring enough coffee? I'm surprised at you, Maris."

"It got stolen," said Benny. "So did the rest of our food. *And* Henry's hiking boots."

"Did you see Bobcat on the trail?" asked Henry.

"Stolen? What? Did Bobcat steal your food and boots?" asked Rayanne, sounding bewildered.

"No, no, no. It's a long story," said Maris. "Come on in."

As Rayanne and Carola drank coffee, the Aldens ate their oatmeal and told the two newcomers everything that had been happening. When they'd finished, Carola said, "Could've been bears that took your food, but it doesn't sound right. It does sound like you've been having a blizzard of bad luck. But then, that goes with this mountain."

"Did you both just hike up the mountain?" asked Henry.

"Yep. Met Carola at the trailhead this morning, near where Maris's truck is parked. She waited until my days off at the diner so I could come with her," Rayanne told them.

"Have you seen any bears?" Violet asked. "We haven't."

Carola looked a little embarrassed. "No," she said shortly.

Everyone was quiet for a moment. Then Rayanne said to Maris, "Is there any reason someone would be out to get you?" she asked.

"No," said Maris firmly.

But Henry said, "We think someone might be trying to scare us away. Keep a trail from being built on Blizzard Mountain."

All four Aldens looked hard at Carola.

"Well, that's interesting," she said.

Rayanne asked, "Did you find any clues? Footprints, for example? You can tell a lot from footprints. The soles of shoes can tell you almost as much as someone's fingerprints, you know."

"No. No footprints," said Jessie regretfully.

Carola put down her coffee cup and stood up. "We'd better get a move on, Rayanne."

To Maris and the Aldens she said, "And we'll keep an eye out for anything suspicious. If someone is trying to scare you away and we find out anything, we'll let you know."

"Have a good hike," Maris said. "I'll walk you to the trail's edge." She and Rayanne headed toward the Blizzard Trail.

Carola stopped at the door to look back at the Aldens.

"If someone is trying to scare you off this mountain, maybe you should leave," she said. "I know I would."

Then she was gone, too.

"Wow," said Henry. "Do you think that was a warning?"

"A warning," said Jessie solemnly, "or a threat."

"Then Carola is the one who's trying to scare us off the mountain?" asked Violet.

"I'm not sure. She could be," said Jessie.

"But she just hiked up here with Rayanne," said Benny.

"That's what she said, Benny. She could have been following us, though. And then hiked *down* to meet Rayanne this morning," Jessie said.

"Unless it's Bobcat who's been trying to scare us," said Henry.

"Or maybe Bobcat and Carola are working together," said Jessie.

"What about Rayanne?" Violet suggested. "She asked a lot of questions."

Benny nodded. "She sounded like one of us. Like a detective."

"I wonder why she's up here. She doesn't even like mountains, remember?" said Henry.

"Maybe she's pretending she doesn't like mountains," Violet said.

"I guess it's possible, Violet," Henry said.

Benny said, "I think it's the treasure. The ghost is trying to keep us away from it."

Henry frowned. "There's no such thing as ghosts," Henry said. "But you might have a point."

"You think it's Stagecoach George, too?" Benny asked, looking very surprised.

Jessie and Violet looked startled, too.

"Maybe not a ghost," said Henry. "But

what if someone has found the treasure, or a clue to the treasure? Maybe it's not a ghost, but a person trying to keep us away."

Jessie's eyes sparkled with sudden excitement. "Maybe you're right, Henry! Remember, in the diner people talked about hikers coming up here to look for the lost treasure. What if someone has found it?"

"But why haven't they taken it?" asked Violet.

"Because it's so heavy. Gold is heavy. Maybe they found it and now they have to come back to get it," said Jessie.

Just then, Maris came back. "Let's get to work," she said. "I think this weather could turn bad any day now. We need to get finished up here and get back down the mountain."

As she walked away, Jessie said to the others, "Maybe we shouldn't tell Maris about what we talked about. We don't want to worry her until we've figured out the mystery."

"Oh," Benny said. "Okay."

"Who's going to help me on the trail?" Maris called.

"I will," said Jessie.

"Since I don't have any shoes, I guess I'll work around the cabin," said Henry.

"Benny and I will stay with you, Henry," said Violet. "And keep you company."

"And look for treasure," said Benny under his breath.

But by late afternoon, the only treasure that had been found was a penny wedged in the floorboards of the cabin and a scrap of purple cloth caught on a splinter of wood near the cabin door. Violet tucked the scrap of purple in her backpack to keep as a souvenir of the trip and Benny put the penny in his pocket.

When Jessie and Maris returned, they were both dusted with snow. Violet showed them the scrap of purple cloth she'd found and Benny told them about his new penny.

Then Jessie said, "I found something, too." She reached in her pocket and pulled out a handful of small, shiny green leaves.

Benny knew what it was at once. "Wintergreen!" he said.

Maris smiled and said, "Right, Benny. We thought we'd use it to make some hot tea to go with dinner."

"Dinner," said Benny at once. "Good!"

After dinner and hot tea, Maris checked to make sure the cabin was locked up tight, windows and doors. Then it was time for bed.

In no time every one of the Aldens had scrambled into a sleeping bag. "I'm going to sleep like a log," Jessie announced.

No one answered. Everyone had fallen fast asleep, just like that.

And a moment later, Jessie did, too.

But no one slept like a log that night.

"OOOOOOOOOOOOOH!" Something wailed right outside the cabin wall.

Jessie bolted up.

"OOOOOOOOOOOOH!"

"Hey! What's that?" Benny said.

Across the room, Maris called out, "Is everyone okay?"

"OOOOOOOOOOOOOH!" The sound

came from the other side of the cabin now.

"The ghost!" cried Benny, sounding scared and excited at the same time.

"A screech owl," said Maris. But her voice was uncertain.

She scrambled out of her sleeping bag and lit one of the candles inside its glass lantern on the table.

Jessie had on one boot and was pulling the other on. Violet was sitting up in her sleeping bag, her eyes wide. Henry was struggling to pull on his thick wool socks.

"OOOOOOOH." The sound came from the back of the cabin. But this time it wasn't so loud. It sounded as if it were fading away.

"That's no screech owl," Jessie said.

"Let's go out there! I want to catch the ghost," Benny said excitedly.

Jessie grabbed her flashlight. "We all do, Benny," she said. "But you can't catch anything but a cold if you go outside in the snow without shoes or a coat."

"Oh, all right," Benny said.

He ran back to his bunk and stuffed his

feet into his boots. By the time he had his coat on, everyone was ready and had their flashlights on. The Aldens raced out of the cabin door into the dark and snowy night.

"Look! Tracks in the snow," said Violet.

They followed the scramble of tracks around the cabin and all over the clearing as well as they could.

Suddenly Jessie pointed. "That way! The tracks go that way!" she said.

Being careful not to step on the tracks, the Aldens followed the tracks to the stream.

"I think I see more tracks on the other side. I'll check," said Jessie. She scrambled nimbly across the rocks while the others waited and watched.

Henry danced from one foot to the other. He could feel the cold snow through his socks. He didn't dare try to follow the others across the icy-cold stream.

How would he ever get back down the trail?

"The tracks stop here," Jessie called from the other side of the water.

"No more tracks?" Henry called back.

"Nope. It's like whoever it was just disappeared," Jessie reported.

Benny nodded wisely. "Ghosts can do that," he said. "Stagecoach George probably just flew away."

"Ghosts don't leave footprints," argued Violet. But she looked around nervously.

Maris shivered. "I agree. Even if there was such a thing as a ghost, no ghost made these tracks. Look at them."

Five flashlights pointed down on the footprints. They were large and deep and smudged along one side.

"Something heavy, with big feet," said Violet, remembering some of the tracking lessons Maris had given them.

"Right, Violet," Maris said. "Heavy weight makes deep tracks. And big footprints mean big feet, which usually means a big person."

Maris knelt and studied the prints some more. "Expensive hiking boots, but not brand-new," she reported. "Someone's been hiking in these for a long time."

"Maybe it's someone small wearing big boots," said Jessie. "Someone small in disguise."

"And it looks like whoever it is might be carrying something heavy," Henry said, forgetting about his own cold, bootless feet for a moment.

"Why?" asked Benny.

"Because the track is uneven," Henry pointed out. "See how it is smudged and blurred on the left side?"

"Another good observation," Maris said. "Someone who's going to be sneaking around in the wilderness in the middle of the night could be carrying a heavy pack with emergency supplies in it."

"And it's either packed unevenly, or somehow it got thrown off balance," Jessie said.

"Right again," said Maris. Suddenly she shivered. "But let's get back inside. I'm getting cold."

Reluctantly, the Aldens returned to the cabin. As they approached, Henry swung his flashlight around the clearing. "The footprints lead into the clearing from the trail," he noted. "And away from the clearing across the stream. And then they stop. How did he — or she — do that?"

"I know!" exclaimed Jessie. "Maybe the person walked backward in his own steps to the stream and then walked up the stream."

"Good idea, Jessie," Maris said. "We'll check around farther up and downstream tomorrow."

"If the snow hasn't covered the tracks," Henry said. "Or — "

But Henry didn't finish what he was about to say. Violet's flashlight beam had stopped on the roof of the cabin.

"Look at that!" Jessie exclaimed.

Henry just stared. He couldn't believe his eyes!

CHAPTER 9

We'll Be Coming Down the Mountain

"Your boots!" shouted Benny. "Look!"

Henry's brown hiking boots were sitting on the cabin roof, right above the door!

Henry walked up to the cabin and stepped onto a stump next to the cabin door. He reached up and took down the boots.

"These are my boots for sure," he said. "And I don't think they've been here long. There's hardly any snow on them."

"But where did they come from?" Violet cried.

"Maybe it's a joke," Benny said.

"I don't think so, Benny," said Henry. "And I don't think it was a ghost."

"Do you think it was whoever was making all that noise?" asked Violet.

"It had to be," said Jessie. She frowned. "But why? Why would anyone take your boots and then bring them back?"

"Maybe the thief realized that Henry couldn't hike back down without his boots," said Benny.

"Oh, no!" gasped Violet. "What if the boot thief took something else?"

They all pushed quickly into the cabin. But nothing had been touched. The cabin was just as they had left it.

"I don't care who took the boots! I've had it," Maris declared. "We're going home tomorrow."

"But what about the trail?" asked Jessie.

"We've done as much on the trail as we need to do before the winter snow sets in. And from the looks of things, if we don't head down the trail soon, winter could trap us here," said Maris.

"But we haven't caught the ghost . . . or the thief yet," said Benny.

"We will," said Jessie.

Maris woke the Aldens before the sun was up the next morning. "It looks like it has been snowing off and on all night," she told them. "We need to get down the mountain while we can."

They ate quickly, then loaded their packs and headed out.

"All the footprints from last night are gone," said Benny.

"Yep. Whoever's been bothering us got lucky," said Henry.

The snow fell and fell as the little group slipped and slid down the side of the mountain. Drifts of snow soon covered the trail and Maris stopped often to make sure that they hadn't lost their way.

Halfway down, Benny sank onto a rock. "My legs are *tired*," he said. "They don't want to walk anymore."

"I could carry you," Henry said.

But Maris shook her head. "Benny's too

heavy for you to carry on this slippery trail," she said. As she spoke, she pulled out the lightweight ax she carried and began to hack at a small tree by the trail.

"What are you doing?" Jessie asked.

"Building a sort of sled to pull Benny on," Maris said. Swiftly she cut another tree. "Trim the branches off that tree and I'll trim this one."

When the branches were trimmed off both trees, Maris cut one trunk exactly in half. Then she cut the other trunk into four pieces. She laid the two long pieces of wood side by side. She tied the four shorter pieces across the two long pieces, in the middle.

"It looks like a ladder," said Benny.

"It does," said Maris. "But it's your new sled."

Quickly Maris wove some of the branches in and out of the rungs of the ladder-sled. Last of all, she lashed her waterproof tarp over the branches.

"Hop on," she told Benny. "And let's go."

Benny climbed onto the sled and grabbed each side. Maris picked up the two poles on the end of the sled facing down the trail and started forward.

"Hold on tight," she said. Benny and the sled slid over the snow.

Henry and Maris took turns pulling Benny. With Benny in the sled, they could all travel much faster.

They reached the bottom of the trail in the late afternoon. They were all very tired.

"Looks like we're the last ones out," said Maris. "Carola's truck is gone and so's Rayanne's car. They must have come out even earlier than we did. I guess the snow buried their footprints."

"Bobcat's truck is gone, too," said Violet.

"At least we know he's not up on the mountain somewhere," said Jessie.

"We'll check in town," said Maris. "I'm sure Bobcat is fine and there's a logical reason why he didn't come back."

"Whew," said Henry, helping Benny climb off the sled. "I was getting worried for a while there that we were going to get stuck on Blizzard Mountain."

"It's a good thing you built me a sled," said Benny to Maris. "Thank you."

"You're welcome, Benny," said Maris. "It's a good way to move something heavy, isn't it? Especially when it snows."

"Sort of like a dogsled," said Jessie.

"Yes," agreed Maris. She smiled tiredly. "It's also a good thing you got your boots back, though, Henry. You would have been a lot heavier to pull!"

They climbed into the truck.

"I'm hungry," Benny announced.

Maris nodded. "Next stop, the diner," she said. "We can get something to eat. And we can ask about Bobcat."

Benny pushed the diner door open. "It smells good!" he said. He raced to the counter to sit down.

"Rayanne!" said Jessie in surprise, as she and the others followed Benny. "Did you hike down Blizzard Mountain this morning and then come to work?"

The silver-haired waitress shook her head. "Nope. We hiked back down last night. Carola didn't like the way the weather looked. Hiking at night. Ha!"

"I guess you didn't like it," said Benny.

"You guessed that right," said the waitress. "What can I get you?"

"Anything but beans," said Benny.

"Has anyone seen Bobcat?" Maris asked abruptly.

"I haven't," said Rayanne. "No one I've talked to has."

"I'm going to go check at the general store and see what I can find out," said Maris. She slid off her counter stool and walked briskly out.

Jessie fixed Rayanne with a solemn look. "You hiked down the mountain last night?" she asked.

"If I go hiking again, it's going to be in the summer," declared Rayanne.

"Next time, you can take that purple opera cape," said Benny.

"What did you say?" Jessie asked.

"Remember that old purple velvet opera cape that got stolen?" he said. "And people were talking about it here and joking that you could use it to fly down the mountain like a superhero?" Benny flapped his arms. "I just remembered that!" He laughed.

"That's it," Jessie whispered. "That's it!"

"What?" asked Violet.

But before Jessie could answer, the door to the diner opened.

Chuck limped in on his crutches.

"You're back," he said to the Aldens. "Did you have a good trip? See any ghosts?"

"Yes," said Benny.

"No," said Henry firmly.

"Not exactly," Jessie added.

"Well, at least you didn't get trapped in all this snow," Chuck said. He bent and knocked snow from his boots. "But I guess a little snow won't hurt these old boots of mine."

"Maybe you should get new boots," said Benny, "to go with all your new hiking stuff."

"New hiking stuff?" Chuck looked at Benny.

"Carola told us when you got lost, it was

because you had all new stuff," Benny said.

Chuck laughed and said, "I think I know what Carola said, and she's right. New gear isn't what makes you a good hiker. You have to learn that, just like lessons in school."

Rayanne put a menu in front of Chuck. He glanced down, then glanced up again. "Where's your friend Bobcat?" he asked the Aldens.

"He's missing," said Jessie. She had a very odd expression on her face.

"Missing?" asked Chuck. He raised his eyebrows. "That's strange. I just saw him a couple of days ago."

"You did?" Violet said, her voice going up in surprise.

"Sure. Outside the general store. He was loading supplies into his truck. Said he was on his way back up the mountain to bring them to you," Chuck said.

"He never hiked back up to bring us those supplies," Henry said.

Chuck stroked his beard as if trying to remember something. Then he said, "You know, now that I think about it, I did wonder why Bobcat did what he did."

"What did Bobcat do?" Violet asked.

"He drove in the wrong direction when he left here," said Chuck. "The opposite direction from Blizzard Mountain."

Jessie jumped up. "Thanks," she said. "Come on, everyone. We have to find Maris." She raced out of the diner.

The other Aldens exchanged surprised looks. Then they followed their sister. They met Maris just outside the door. "Bobcat's okay," Jessie said.

"What? How do you know that?" Maris asked.

"How do you know?" asked Henry at the same time.

"Jessie?" Violet said.

"Do you know where Bobcat is?" asked Benny.

"Not exactly, but I'm sure he's okay. Come on! And I have a plan to catch the ghost that's been trying to scare us all off Blizzard Mountain," Jessie said. "This is what we need to do — and why."

* * *

The Aldens walked back into the diner a few minutes later. "Back so soon?" Rayanne asked.

"We're going to call Grandfather. He's at Maris's cabin. We hope he can drive into Blizzard Gap to meet us for dinner," explained Henry.

"The phone booth is in the hall. I'll be right back," said Maris.

The Aldens settled down at a table.

Chuck chewed the hamburger he had ordered. He nodded to the Aldens, then said, "Did you find Bobcat yet?"

"We will. Tomorrow," said Jessie. "But we can't look for him now. It's too dark."

"I'm sure he's okay," Chuck said. "Maybe he had an emergency and had to leave in a hurry."

"Yes. That's what probably happened," agreed Jessie. She turned to Violet and said in a loud voice, "Show me that piece of cloth you found at the cabin, Violet."

Violet reached into her pocket and pulled out the small scrap of purple cloth.

"Velvet," said Jessie. "Purple velvet."

"It looks old," said Benny.

"Probably been stuck up in the cabin for years," said Henry. He made sure the others in the diner could hear their conversation.

"Velvet's a funny thing to find in an old cabin in the woods, don't you think, Violet?" Jessie asked.

"You're right," said Violet.

"Maybe it's a clue," said Benny. "To buried treasure."

Rayanne was standing behind the counter, motionless. Her eyes were fixed on the scrap of velvet Violet held. "Where did you find that?" she demanded.

"Up at the cabin," said Violet. "Isn't it pretty?"

Rayanne came around the counter and snatched up the bit of velvet. She stared at it, then slapped it down on the table. She went back to work without another word.

But the Aldens felt her sharp eyes watching them.

Chuck dropped his hamburger and

ketchup splashed on his shirt. He grabbed a napkin and begin to poke at the stain.

"Yes, it is a clue," Benny said, in a louder voice than before. "I bet it's a clue to where Stagecoach George hid his treasure."

"In the cabin? Oh, Benny, do you think so?" said Violet.

"I do," said Benny.

"Well, we should go up there and look," said Henry. "Maybe Maris will take us up tomorrow."

Now Chuck dropped the napkin. He bent over to pick it up and straightened. He hit his head on the table. "Ow!" he said.

"Tomorrow. First thing. We go on a treasure hunt," said Jessie.

"But . . . but . . . what about Bobcat?" asked Chuck.

"We'll find the treasure. And maybe Bobcat, too," said Benny, smiling. "We're *very* good at finding things. Ask anybody back in Greenfield."

Maris came back into the diner. "Your grandfather's on his way," she said.

"Good," said Henry. "We can tell him about this clue we found."

Violet held up the piece of velvet and nodded. "And about the ghost and how he tried to scare us away and didn't," she said. "And about how we're going to hike right back up Blizzard Mountain to that cabin and look for treasure."

CHAPTER 10

How to Catch a Ghost

"I'm glad it stopped snowing," whispered Violet.

"Me, too. And when the sun comes up, it'll be warmer," said Jessie.

They were huddled in the little lean-to just off the Blizzard Trail. They'd been there since right before dawn. From where they sat, they could see the trail clearly.

"It didn't turn out to be much of a snow-storm after all," Benny complained.

"Shhh, everyone!" Henry warned.

After that, the Aldens were quiet.

"What if this doesn't work?" Violet said very, very softly.

"Maris is waiting just down the trail at the next big rock," Henry reminded her. "One way or another, our trap will work."

"Listen . . ." Benny said.

They all grew quiet now. And then they heard it. Something was scraping over snow. Someone was coming down the Blizzard Trail.

Crunch, crunch, crunch went the sound of boots on thin snow.

There was also the sound of something heavy being pulled over that same thin snow. *Swish, bump, bump, swish.*

A figure appeared through the trees. Everyone held their breath.

The figure leaned forward and pulled hard on a rope in one hand. A sled bumped along at the end of the rope. "Whoa," the figure commanded, and raised one foot awkwardly to slow down the sled.

"Let's go," said Jessie, and leaped to her feet and out of the lean-to.

The person saw the four Aldens running

through the trees and, yanking the sled hard, began to run, too.

"Stop!" cried Jessie.

"Stop, thief!" shouted Benny. Henry jumped forward — and landed right on the sled.

The sled tipped over. The person pulling the sled stumbled and fell, but tried to get up and run again.

But by this time Maris had stepped out into the middle of the trail.

"Give up, Chuck," said Henry. "We know all about the gold."

The man turned and pushed the hood of his jacket back. Chuck's face was red.

"What a dumb thing I did," he said, and sat down hard on a fallen tree trunk.

Jessie stepped forward and pulled back the tarp on the sled. Underneath was a lump, covered with purple velvet. Carefully, she and Violet lifted the velvet cape. Gold bars shone beneath it.

"Gold!" said Benny.

"It's the museum gold," said Violet.

"I . . . I . . . oh, no," moaned Chuck, and buried his face in his hands.

"Not exactly gold," said a new voice.

Maris and the Aldens looked up in surprise at the woman striding up the trail.

"Rayanne?" asked Maris. "What are *you* doing here?"

"Rayanne Adams, private detective, at your service," said Rayanne.

"But you work at the diner!" said Violet.

"That's because I was undercover. What better place to find out what's going on than at the town's only diner?" asked Rayanne. She stared at Chuck. "You ought to be ashamed of yourself, mister, robbing that museum."

"I didn't mean to." Chuck looked up. "I was just standing there, and no one was around, and I saw how easy it would be to take the gold that was on display. I put a piece of tape on the back door lock and just pushed the door open right after the museum closed. I wrapped the gold in that old purple cape and carried it out."

"You're a private detective?" Maris asked Rayanne.

Rayanne nodded. "My nephew runs the museum. I'm retired now, but I agreed to take this case to help him out."

"That's why you asked so many questions! And knew so much about the museum theft!" cried Jessie.

"Yep," said Rayanne. "And I had my suspicions about Mr. Chuck Larson here. But until you came along, I couldn't prove anything. How did you know to make a trap for him?"

"Two clues," said Henry. "Shoes and purple velvet. Chuck was acting like a hiker who didn't know anything. But he wore good old comfortable hiking boots. Boots that had been used a lot."

"And they were worn down on one side, like a man who'd been limping while wearing them," said Jessie. "That matched the boot prints we found in the snow. The prints weren't very clear, but they were clear enough to show us that whoever walked around our cabin limped on the same foot as Chuck. Only we didn't know *why* he'd be following us."

"We thought first he'd found Stagecoach George's treasure. It wasn't until you mentioned the cape from the museum was purple velvet and we remembered that scrap of purple cloth Violet had found that things began to make sense," said Henry.

"That purple velvet was an important clue," Rayanne agreed. "It got my attention. And it got Chuck's attention, too."

"That's when we knew for sure Chuck was faking it. That his ankle was not all that broken anymore," said Benny.

Henry looked at Chuck. "You're not even a history teacher, are you? It was all faked."

Chuck groaned. "No," he confessed. "I'm a mountain guide from out West. I came here just to hike."

"We should have known you were no beginner when we found you all snug in your tent when you were injured. Beginners usually wander off the trail. And they aren't so prepared," said Maris.

"I was hoping you wouldn't notice that," Chuck said. "Anyway, I'd carried the gold, wrapped in the cape, in my pack, about halfway down Blizzard Mountain when I slipped and broke my ankle." He made a face at the memory.

"I knew I was near the cabin — I'd used it on the way over the mountain the first time. So I managed to get there and bury the gold under the floor of the cabin and put the boards back down."

"That's why there was so much dirt on the floor," said Violet. "We figured that out, too."

He nodded. "I guess that's when a piece of purple velvet tore off that old cape. Anyway, I dragged myself back over to the trail so no one would know I'd been in the cabin. I had enough supplies to last awhile, and I knew I'd be okay, that someone would come along before long."

"You let the air out of our tires, too," Benny accused Chuck.

"Yes, it was me. When I went to the bathroom at the diner, I really sneaked out and did that. And I followed you up the trail and took part of your food," Chuck confessed. "I hoped that would scare you off, but it didn't. So I followed you to the cabin and tried to scare you away then."

"And you took my boots," said Henry.

"I did. But I gave them back!" said Chuck. "I couldn't let you try to hike down the mountain without them, any more than I could leave you without any food at all. I'm a mountain guide. I just couldn't do it."

"You're a better mountain guide than a thief," said Rayanne. "That wasn't even gold that you took."

Chuck sat up. "What?" he said.

"Iron bars painted to look like gold, for the mining display," said Rayanne. "That's all it is. Heavy and worthless. It's the cape the museum wants back. It's an important part of this park's history."

Chuck's mouth had fallen open. So had Benny's.

"N-not gold?" Chuck managed to stammer at last.

"Nope," said Rayanne. "So now that

we've got the cape back, the museum's going to let you go."

"You will?" said Chuck. He jumped to his feet. "Oh, thank you! I'll never, ever do something like that again. I've never done anything like that before. I know it was wrong. I've learned my lesson."

"Good," said Jessie. She almost felt sorry for Chuck.

"Thank you," Chuck cried again. "Thank you."

"Go on, then," said Rayanne. "We'll get this down the mountain."

Chuck looked around. Then, almost running, he headed down the mountain.

As the Aldens and Maris and Rayanne came out of the woods at the bottom of the Blizzard Trail, Grandfather Alden stepped out of a car parked near Maris's truck.

"Grandfather!" said Jessie. "We caught the thief."

"And Rayanne's a real live detective," said Benny.

Another person got out of the truck.

"Bobcat!" said Maris. "There you are. What happened?"

"We forgot to ask Chuck what he told you to make you leave town," said Henry.

"So you figured it out, huh?" Bobcat chuckled. He shook his head. "And I fell for it, too. Chuck met me outside the general store. Must have been waiting for me, I realize now. He gave me a message, said it had been left at the diner for me. That's not unusual. Everyone knows that the people at the diner can always find you. It's the way a small town works."

"What was the message?" asked Violet.

"My brother had an attack of appendicitis. It said please come at once. Chuck said he'd see that someone else took supplies to you, so I drove to the airport and flew halfway across the country. Boy, was my brother surprised to see me. We had a nice visit, though." Bobcat grinned. "That buzzard!"

"Bobcat called when he got back," Grandfather explained. "I told him what had been going on and we drove here."

"But what about when your truck

wouldn't start, Maris? Did Chuck do that, too?" asked Violet.

"Nope. My truck's just an old truck. But Chuck knew about the trouble I'd been having with it. Carola had stopped by the diner earlier on her way out of town and been talking about it. That's what gave him the idea to try to scare us off the trail until he could get back up there and haul the gold out," said Maris.

"And because his ankle was hurting, he waited until the first snow so it would be easy to pull the gold out by sled. Only it wasn't gold," Henry concluded.

"Chuck made a mistake," said Rayanne. "And he got caught. Bad luck for Chuck."

"He always said Blizzard Mountain was a bad luck mountain," Bobcat said. "Looks like it was — for him."

"But good luck for us," said Benny.

Everyone looked at Benny. "What do you mean, Benny?" asked Jessie.

"Well, Stagecoach George's gold is still up on Blizzard Mountain," Benny said. "So on our next visit, we can go back and find it!"

THE MYSTERY AT SNOWFLAKE INN

created by
GERTRUDE CHANDLER WARNER

Illustrated by Charles Tang

ALBERT WHITMAN & Company
Chicago, Illinois

The Mystery at Snowflake Inn
created by Gertrude Chandler Warner;
illustrated by Charles Tang.

ISBN 10: 0-8075-5346-8
ISBN 13: 978-0-8075-5346-6

For more information about Albert Whitman & Company,
please visit our web site at www.albertwhitman.com.

Contents

Contents

CHAPTER 1

The Old Inn in the Woods

"This is it, Grandfather!" Henry Alden said, examining a map. "Turn left on White Pine Road."

"You're a good guide!" James Alden said.

Being fourteen, Henry knew he should be able to read a map. Still, he was pleased at Grandfather's praise.

Behind Henry were Jessie and Violet, his sisters, and in the back seat, his brother, six-year-old Benny. Next to Benny sat Soo Lee. The little Korean girl was just a year older than Benny and always liked to be with him.

"Soo Lee," Benny said, "I'm glad you could come with us on our winter holiday."

"Yes, indeed," said Grandfather. He knew how much Joe and Alice Alden, their cousins, loved their adopted daughter, and how they hated to be parted from her. But they also wanted Soo Lee to have an old-fashioned New England holiday.

Benny gazed out the back window, his eyes widening as James Alden steered the van onto a narrow road lined with trees on both sides. A sparkling snow blanket covered the hilly land. "I like Vermont!" Benny said, his round face breaking into a smile. "I've never stayed at an old inn before."

Violet, who was ten, returned his smile. "And it's *very* old, Benny. The inn was built when George Washington lived!"

"Wow," Benny whispered. "That's *really* old!"

"Won't it be fun to spend the holidays here?" Jessie asked.

James Alden laughed as the van bumped over a rut. "I thought you children might like to ride in a sleigh pulled by horses, ice skate on a pond, and . . ."

"And hike through the woods," Henry added, folding the map and slipping it into the glove compartment.

They drove past a frozen pond with snow geese clustered nearby.

As they rounded a curve, Jessie gasped at the sight before her eyes. "The inn! How beautiful!" Nestled among the fir trees, the colonial inn looked as white as the snow. White ruffled curtains decorated the many windows and a white sign swung from a post. It read:

SNOWFLAKE INN

1767

"Snowflake Inn," Violet said. "How pretty."

Jessie glanced at Violet. "I hope you brought your paints."

Violet nodded, pleased that her older sister thought she could paint this old inn. Her sketch pad would be the first thing she'd unpack.

Benny pointed to gray smoke drifting up to the blue sky. "Look! Smoke is coming out of the chimney. Do you think there's a fireplace?"

"I'm sure of it!" Grandfather said with a chuckle, as he drove up the circular drive. He stopped before a wide door with a huge wreath tied with a red ribbon.

A patch of color showed through the snow-covered roof. "That red roof reminds me of our red boxcar," Benny said.

"I like the story about where you once lived," Soo Lee said. "You thought your grandfather was mean and you ran away from him." She gave James Alden an impish look.

"We were very wrong," Violet said.

"I'll tell you, though," Henry said, opening the door, "this inn sure looks a lot more comfortable than our boxcar."

"We did make our boxcar cozy, though," Violet said.

"We cooked and cleaned and made it our home," agreed Jessie.

"Yes, you did a good job of living on your

own," Mr. Alden said. "But I'm glad I found you."

"I'm glad, too," Benny said, hopping out of the car. His boots made a crunching sound on the snow.

Soo Lee jumped lightly to the ground behind him.

Benny moved to his grandfather's side. "You're the best grandfather in the whole world."

"Yes, you are," twelve-year-old Jessie said, carrying her suitcase up the brick walk.

"I agree, too," Violet said shyly, following Jessie.

"That makes four of us," Henry said, grabbing two suitcases.

"I like you, also, Mr. . . . " Soo Lee echoed softly.

James threw back his head and laughed. "Please, Soo Lee, call me Grandfather, won't you?"

Soo Lee nodded, giving Mr. Alden a big smile.

Benny took Grandfather's hand, skipping beside the tall, straight-shouldered gentleman. "This is going to be fun!"

Suddenly the door opened and a gray-haired man greeted them. He leaned on a cane, and, although he appeared frail, his voice was steady and strong. "Welcome to Snowflake Inn. You must be the Aldens. I've been waiting for you. I'm Ralph Winston, the owner. Just come this way." His walk was slow because of a slight limp. "After you put your suitcases in the rooms with your names on the doors, I want to show you my inn." He turned and a smile lit his wrinkled face.

Going upstairs, Violet felt the banister wobble under her hand and heard the stairs creak under her boots. The inn looked as if nothing had been done to it for 200 years!

Violet, Jessie, and Soo Lee entered their large room and unpacked. Next door, Henry and Benny hung up their clothes, while down the hall, in his own room, James Alden placed shirts and pants in a drawer.

When everyone was ready, they met Mr. Winston downstairs in the parlor.

"We'll begin our tour of this fine inn right

here," Mr. Winston said. "I've tried to keep it just as it was in 1767."

"I believe it," Jessie murmured, staring up at the beamed ceiling and the peeling wallpaper.

"Dad!" a man of about thirty burst into the room. "The kitchen is a disaster! I've fixed the leaky faucets, but Greta is complaining. She's a good cook and deserves a new stove!" His black eyes flashed, fastening on the older man's face. "Now the sink is cracked. We need a new one!"

"No!" Mr. Winston said firmly. "Leave the sink as it is!"

The young man glared. "This whole place is falling apart!" His black curly hair and short black beard fairly bristled. "I hope it falls down around your ears!"

Benny bit his lip, not daring to breathe. Maybe this vacation wasn't going to be as much fun as he'd thought.

CHAPTER 2

Unfriendly Guests

For a moment the only sound was the ticking of the grandfather clock in the corner. Then Mr. Winston said, "This is my son, Larry."

Larry's features softened and he smiled.

"Meet the Aldens," Ralph Winston said. "Jessie, Violet, Henry, James Alden, Soo Lee, and Benny."

Benny stuck out his hand. "I'm pleased to meet you, Larry Winston."

Larry Winston bent down and graciously shook Benny's hand. "Call me Larry.

Please." He straightened. "You'll have to for-
give Dad and me. We're having a constant
battle about this inn. I want to modernize it
and Dad insists it's fine just the way it is."
Larry sighed, looking about. "No television,
no phones. I don't mind the TV, but we
should have a phone. Snowflake Inn is
uncomfortable."

Mr. Winston frowned. "It's not uncomfortable!"

Larry shrugged, holding up his hands.
"It's your inn, Dad. I give up." He turned
to leave. "I'll see you all later." With his fist,
he lightly hit Benny's shoulder. "Maybe we
can put together a jigsaw puzzle."

"Yes," Benny said. "I'd like that."

"Well, that's another argument over with,"
Mr. Winston said, shaking his head and
watching as Larry closed the door. "Now,
let me tell you about this fireplace." With his
cane he pointed out the black marble fireplace, surrounded by white wood and a
wooden mantel. The worn colonial sofas,
placed on each side of the roaring fire, held
needlepoint pillows.

Benny yawned. He hoped Mr. Winston wasn't going to tell them about every antique chair, every lamp, and every table.

They all followed Mr. Winston back to Grandfather's room. Ralph Winston pointed to the large bed. "George Washington stayed overnight at this inn," he paused dramatically, "and he slept in this very bed."

Benny touched a square on the quilt, gazing in awe at the footstool needed to climb into the high bed. "George Washington slept *here?*"

"It's hard to believe, isn't it?" Henry said. "I want to take a picture of this four-poster bed before we leave. If that's okay, Mr. Winston?"

"Call me Ralph." Mr. Winston chuckled, pleased. "Take all the pictures you want."

On the tour, they went through each small, low-ceilinged room with their different shapes. Some were long and narrow. Some were square. As they moved from room to room, the wooden floors creaked.

Benny liked the fireplaces in each bed-

room. Violet admired the old portraits. Henry could have spent the rest of the afternoon in the library. In the dining room, Grandfather examined an antique china cabinet, filled with blue-and-white dishes. Jessie was impressed with the crystal chandelier and the small shade on every electric candle. In the sunny kitchen, Soo Lee pointed to a porcelain rooster. Of everything she'd seen, this was her favorite.

"Hello!" boomed a voice behind them. A woman came bustling in, carrying a bag of onions. "I'm Greta Erickson, the cook."

"And a mighty fine one she is, too!" Ralph Winston said. "She's known for her delicious desserts. Wait until you taste her chocolate cake." He introduced everyone.

Greta winked at the children. "It's a wonder I can cook anything on that ancient stove! It's a wood-burning one!" She shook her head. Soo Lee looked up at Greta. She'd never seen such a tall woman. Thick braids on top of her head made her look even taller.

"You really do love this inn, don't you, Mr. Winston?" Henry asked.

"I sure do. But I'm getting too old to handle it. I'm going to have to retire soon," Ralph Winston said, with an air of regret.

Benny hoped the kitchen was the last room on the tour. He wanted to explore on his own. Ralph, however, held up his hand and said in a low tone, "I have one more place to show you. It's a mysterious nook and has quite a history."

"What is it?" Benny asked in an eager voice.

Ralph, a finger to his lips, hobbled quietly out of the kitchen toward the back stairs. There he stopped.

Puzzled, Benny stared at the brick wall beneath the stairs. "Is this it?" he asked in a disappointed voice.

Ralph Winston chuckled. "That's right, James." And with his cane he pressed against a brick. Slowly, a door opened.

"Wow! A hidden door!" Henry said, peering into the darkness.

"There's no light here, but I've hung a lantern inside." Ralph struck a match and lit the wick, revealing a tiny room.

Jessie edged forward. "A secret room," she marveled, gazing about. She couldn't stand upright because of the slanting stairway overhead.

"What is it for?" Violet questioned, ducking her head and looking inside.

Ralph answered, "During the Revolutionary War, when we fought the British for our freedom, Mr. Whitley, the owner of Snowflake Inn hid Colonial spies in this very nook."

"Wow," Benny said.

"Yessirree," Ralph went on. "He hid Americans who were sneaking secret messages through British lines. The coded messages told the Colonial forces about British troop movements and the size of their regiments. Sometimes, though, these spies were betrayed and had to flee from the Redcoats. If they had been caught, they would have been shot as traitors."

"Redcoats?" Soo Lee asked.

"The British were nicknamed 'Redcoats,'" Henry explained, "because their uniforms had bright red jackets."

"Was George Washington in the war?" Soo Lee asked, her small oval face, framed by short black hair, tilted to one side.

"He was the leading general for the Americans," Violet replied.

Benny stepped inside the tiny niche. "This is a neat hiding place," he said.

Ralph, pleased with himself, smiled. "I thought you might like it. Someday I'll tell you the story of Madge Carson and her daughter." He nodded. "Her daughter, Penelope, was just about your age, Benny."

"Was Madge a spy?" Benny asked, coming out in the open.

"She was one of the best," Ralph responded, "but I'll save that tale for a snowy day. Right now, Greta is serving cake in the dining room." He pressed a brick, and the door swung shut.

Just then, a young woman, dressed in jeans and a jacket, hurried past them.

"Betsy!" Ralph said, "I want you to meet our new guests."

Impatiently, the woman pulled on her gloves. "I'm Betsy Calvert," she said.

"My niece," Ralph said, introducing the Aldens and Soo Lee. "Isn't Betsy a perfect name for someone staying in this old inn?"

"Betsy?" Soo Lee asked.

"Betsy Ross," Ralph said. "She sewed the first American flag."

"Oh, I see," Soo Lee replied. "Thank you."

"I'm pleased to meet you," Betsy said with a frown. She turned to her uncle. "Uncle Ralph, the window in my room is stuck. I can't budge it up or down."

"I'll fix it," Ralph said.

Benny wrinkled his nose, sniffing. He leaned toward Betsy. "You smell good!" he announced.

Violet caught the jasmine scent also, but it was too sweet for her taste.

Betsy stopped and stared at Benny. When she spoke, she said stiffly, "Thank you." Then she brushed by him, and was gone.

Ralph has a very unfriendly niece, thought Jessie. She hoped they wouldn't run into Betsy often.

No sooner had Betsy left when the back

door burst open and a boy and girl about Violet's age dashed through the kitchen and rudely past them.

"That's Davey and Hannah Miller," Ralph said after they'd gone. "They've only been here two days and all they do is complain, or get into trouble. They can't find anything to do, except make mischief, and they want to go home." He smiled at the children. "Maybe now that you've arrived, you can cheer them up."

Violet had her doubts. Poor Mr. Winston. His niece was unfriendly, his son angry and argumentative, and two of his guests wanted to leave. She glanced at Henry. Was he thinking what she was? With some people, no matter how hard you tried, nothing made them happy.

CHAPTER 3

Almost a Sleigh Ride

Before their first dinner at Snowflake Inn, Violet dressed with care, in a striped lavender shirt and purple pants.

"I see you're wearing your favorite colors," Jessie said, as she brushed her long brown hair until it shone.

Violet nodded. "What's your favorite color, Soo Lee?"

"Red," the girl answered instantly.

"Then I think you should have something red," Jessie said, taking a crimson ribbon and tying a bow in Soo Lee's hair.

Pleased, Soo Lee studied herself in the mirror. "Thank you, Jessie."

"We'd better go downstairs," Violet said. "We don't want to be late for dinner."

Mr. Alden met his grandchildren at the head of the stairs and nodded approvingly at their appearance. Benny had slicked back his hair and Henry wore a navy sweater and tan trousers.

Grandfather looked pleased as they entered the dining room.

A pewter tea service, crystal goblets, tall candles, and a blazing fire in the fireplace made the blue room gleam in the soft light.

Larry Winston and Betsy Calvert were seated side by side, and a couple with their two children sat together.

Ralph Winston made certain everyone knew each other. Steven and Rose Miller were the parents of Davey, eight, and Hannah, ten. Henry remembered the Millers' son and daughter by their red hair, which he'd seen earlier. The two had inherited their hair color from Mr. Miller who had an orange fringe around his bald head.

Jessie smiled at the Miller children, and hoped they'd join in the fun at the inn. But by their angry expressions, she wasn't sure they'd want to.

Mr. Winston rang a small silver bell, and Greta entered with a covered bowl.

With a flourish the cook lifted off the lid. "Beef stew!" she crowed. "The meat finally got done. No thanks to that old stove!"

"It smells delicious," Violet said, placing her napkin in her lap.

"And looks yummy," Benny added, rubbing his stomach. "I'm hungry!"

"When aren't you hungry?" Henry said with a chuckle.

Soo Lee passed a platter to Betsy. "Would you like some carrots, Betsy Ross?" she asked.

Davey's freckled face broke into a wide grin, and Hannah stifled a giggle.

"It's not Betsy Ross!" Betsy corrected irritably. "It's Betsy Calvert!"

"I'm sorry," Soo Lee apologized. Her lower lip trembled.

"It's all right," Jessie said. "Look, here are some pickled apples." She put one on Soo Lee's plate. "You'll like them."

Soo Lee returned her smile. Jessie made everything all right again.

Mr. Miller put down his fork and said in a cheerful voice, "Tomorrow you'll have a good time, Davey. Do you know the surprise that's planned?"

Davey shrugged. "I don't care. I just wish we weren't here!"

Rose Miller put on a smile. "Wouldn't you like to ride in a horse-drawn sleigh?"

Davey shrugged. "I guess so."

Hannah played with her potatoes. "Maybe a sleigh ride would be okay, but it's just so boring here."

"You can say that again!" Davey said. "Why couldn't we have gone to an amusement park instead?"

"We thought you'd like an old-fashioned holiday," her mother said.

"Snowflake Inn is such an historic place!" Steven Miller said. "Isn't it exciting that

George Washington stayed here?"

Unimpressed, Davey took a deep breath, gazing at the ceiling.

"I think a sleigh ride will be fun," Benny piped up. "We can sing as we go."

Throwing down his napkin, Davey said, "I'm going to my room."

Rose bit her lip. "All right, dear, but don't you want a piece of Greta's chocolate cake?"

"No," Davey said, standing.

It was too bad Davey was so unhappy, Violet thought. She wondered how they could cheer him up. She wished Hannah would be her friend. She was just her age. But how could you make friends with someone so grouchy?

When dinner was finished, Ralph Winston challenged Grandfather to a chess game.

Larry brought out a jigsaw puzzle, and the Alden children settled around a table before the fireplace. Violet beckoned to Hannah, pointing to an empty chair beside her.

Slowly Hannah sat down, and for a while seemed to enjoy herself. But when Davey called to her from the head of the stairs, she quickly leaped up, moving to the doorway.

"Let's meet in the morning at the stable for the sleigh ride," Violet called.

Hannah paused. "Is ten o'clock okay?"

Violet said, "That's fine. We'll be there."

Maybe Hannah and Davey just needed a few friends their own age, Violet thought.

Soon Benny's eyelids grew heavy and his head drooped forward.

Jessie stretched. She was tired, too. It had been a long day. The children said good night to Larry, Ralph, and Grandfather, and went to bed.

In the morning, after a breakfast of sausages and Greta's Swedish pancakes with delicious Vermont maple syrup, the children put on their jackets, mittens, and knit caps.

"I can't wait!" Benny said. "Won't a ride in the snow be fun?"

"It's not ten o'clock yet, but we can go out and wait for the others," Jessie said.

"Let's go," Benny said impatiently, tugging at Henry's jacket.

Henry laughed, lifting Benny up on his shoulders. "We're off on a sleigh ride!"

When the Aldens arrived at the stable, Hannah and Davey were already waiting.

They certainly got here early, Jessie thought.

Suddenly Larry hurried out from the stable. "The horses!" he exclaimed. "The horses are missing!"

Benny's mouth dropped open. "The horses are *gone?* Did they run away?"

"Someone left the stall door open and let them out!" Larry said grimly.

"You mean a person deliberately let the horses go free?" Henry asked with a frown.

Violet glanced at Hannah and Davey and was puzzled to see that they didn't look at all surprised. It was almost as if they'd known all along the horses were gone. "Let's go in, Hannah," Davey said as he got to his feet. "I knew something would happen to ruin the day!"

Jessie stared after the Millers as they walked slowly up the path. Who would have let the horses out on purpose. And why?

CHAPTER 4

Missing Horses!

Mystified, Larry Winston rubbed his neatly trimmed beard. "I can't figure out why anyone would do this."

"Will the horses come back?" Benny asked in a worried tone. "I hope they're not hurt."

"I'm certain Dobbin and Robin are fine," Larry said. He noticed all the anxious expressions. "It's all right. I have a good idea where the horses probably went."

"Not very far, I hope," Henry said.

"No, not far at all," Larry answered. "Just over at Brian McDowell's farm. About two miles from here on Apple Tree Road." He climbed into his jeep. "Brian will bring them back in his horse trailer." He waved. "I'll be back soon." He turned on the engine and started down the lane.

"Let's look around and see if any clues have been left," Jessie said.

"Clues?" Soo Lee questioned.

"Something that the person who freed the horses left behind," Jessie explained.

Violet and Jessie searched the stable, but they found nothing.

Henry and Soo Lee checked the ground around the barn.

Benny found nothing, too.

"Henry," Soo Lee said, "there are footprints here in the fresh snow."

Henry moved to her side.

Benny hurried over to look, also. "What a lot of footprints!"

"Yes," Henry replied. "And I don't think Larry made them all."

"See," Soo Lee said, stooping. "There's a picture in each footprint."

Henry chuckled. "There is a picture, Soo

Lee, but it's called a pattern or design." He sat on his haunches, studying the footprints. "Inside the heel is a pattern like a small horseshoe."

"I think it's shaped like a wishbone," Benny said, leaning over, hands on his knees.

When the girls came out of the stable, Benny showed them what Soo Lee had discovered.

"You've found a wonderful clue, Soo Lee," Violet said, squeezing the little girl's hand. "You'll make a good detective."

Soo Lee beamed. "Thank you."

"Now we need to keep a sharp lookout for whoever wears boots with heels like that," Jessie said.

"We're all dressed in our warm clothes," Henry said. "Let's not go in. What can we do outdoors?"

"We can play tag," Jessie suggested.

"Or Fox and Geese," Benny added. "That's like tag."

"Yes," Violet said. "You need snow to form a big circle." Violet pointed to a large patch of untrampled snow. "There's the perfect place."

"Oh, good," Soo Lee said, clapping her hands. "This will be fun. We have snow in Korea, but I've never played Fox and Geese."

"I'll run in and get Davey and Hannah," Benny offered. "I'll bet they'd like to play."

"Okay, Benny," Henry said, although he doubted that the Miller children would join in.

But Henry's eyes widened when Benny came out with Davey and Hannah.

First, the children dashed around, forming a big circle by trampling down the snow. Then they made paths up to the center, which was the safe zone. When the circle was completed it resembled a big wheel with spokes.

Jessie was "It," and chased first Soo Lee, then Benny, then Violet, then Henry, then Davey, and finally Hannah. They were the "geese," and they always seemed to land in the safe center, no matter how fast Jessie ran.

At last Jessie tagged Henry. Now, he became "It." For an hour the children zigged and zagged, trying not to be caught.

After Henry tagged Violet, she was "It," and chased after Davey. Davey yelled as he dashed around the circle. Suddenly, the young boy slipped and fell. Violet rushed to help him to his feet. She lifted him and brushed snow from his ski jacket.

Hurrying over to aid her brother, Hannah laughed as she dusted snow from Davey's cap and hair. "You're covered from head to foot."

Davey pushed the girls away. "I'm tired of this silly old game. I'm not playing anymore!" A frown crossed his round face which was covered with even more freckles than his sister's. He stepped out of the circle.

"I think it's time for hot chocolate," Jessie said, trying to soothe Davey's feelings.

"Yes! Yes!" Benny agreed, stamping his feet to keep warm. "I'm cold. Hot chocolate in my pink cup will taste good."

"Your poor chipped cup from our boxcar days," Violet said. "I can't believe it's not broken into a hundred pieces."

"I take good care of it," Benny said. "I

wouldn't want to break my favorite cup."

"I know, Benny," Henry said, throwing his arm around Benny's shoulders. "Let's go up to the inn." He looked back. "Coming, Davey?"

"I guess so," the little boy answered, kicking at the snow.

In the cozy kitchen, Greta filled cups with hot chocolate. She took the tray of cups and a plate of cookies into the living room and put them on a low oak table before the fireplace.

Hannah, Davey, and Violet sat on the sofa, while Henry and Jessie made themselves comfortable in two armchairs on each side of the fire. Benny and Soo Lee sat cross-legged before the yellow flames.

"Hmmm," Benny said, sipping his chocolate, "this is a nice place." He glanced at Davey. "Don't you think so, Davey?"

"It's okay," Davey said, "but it's very different from where we live!"

Hannah gave a nod of agreement.

"Where are you from?" Violet asked politely.

"Boston!" Davey replied.

"That's a big place!" Benny said.

"It's one of the best cities in the world," Hannah said, smiling.

"Outside of Greenfield, Massachusetts," Benny said.

"There's always something to do in Boston!" Davey said.

"I'm sure Boston is fun," Benny said. "But Vermont is fun, too!"

Henry said with a grin, "Benny, no matter where we go, you find something to like."

"I like it here, too," Soo Lee said, a smile brightening her face.

Violet placed the empty cups on the tray and asked, "Who wants to play a game of Monopoly?"

Benny's arm shot straight up. "Me, me!"

Soo Lee giggled, holding up her arm. "Me, me."

"I'll get the board," Jessie said.

"I wonder where Grandfather is," Henry said. "He promised to play a game of chess with me." He headed for the den. "See you later."

Hannah dealt out the play money and the game began.

By the time the game had a winner, with Jessie owning most of the property and money, it was almost lunchtime.

Benny jumped up when he heard the honking of a horn. "Larry's back with the horses!"

"Let's go outside and meet him," Violet said.

Hastily, the children slipped into their jackets, and ran outside.

Larry waved, climbing out of his jeep.

Benny peered down the road and all around, but he didn't see any horses. "Where are Dobbin and Robin?" he asked.

Where are the horses? Violet wondered. Had Larry been wrong about where the horses had gone? She took a breath, feeling scared. As she gazed about at the long faces, she knew she wasn't the only one. Where were the missing horses? Was something wrong?

CHAPTER 5

More Trouble at Snowflake Inn

"Where are the horses?" Benny asked as Larry Winston approached them.

"They're not lost," Larry reassured him. "Dobbin and Robin were right where I said they'd be — in Brian McDowell's meadow. But before Brian can load the horses, he needs to round up a cow that jumped the fence. So instead of going on a sleigh ride now, how would you like to go tonight in the moonlight?"

Benny smiled. "Great!"

"How about it, kids? Does a moonlight ride sound okay?" Larry asked.

"Yes!" everyone chorused. Davey and Hannah nodded, but they didn't look very excited.

On the back porch, Greta jangled a big bell.

"Lunch! We're coming, Greta!" Larry called. "I'm starved. How about you, Davey?" He messed up Davey's red hair.

Davey nodded. "I could eat."

"The cold sure gave me an appetite," Henry said, following Larry inside.

"Me, too," Benny agreed.

Soon, a delicious lunch of chili, corn bread, salad, and coconut cream pie was devoured. Greta chuckled to see how fast her food disappeared.

After eating, Soo Lee leaned back in her chair, closing her eyes. "I ate a lot."

"How about a nap?" Violet asked.

Soo Lee rubbed her eyes, yawning. "Yes, I'm sleepy!"

So Soo Lee curled up on the sofa, Jessie and Hannah played checkers, Davey and

Benny worked a new jigsaw puzzle, Henry read, and Violet sketched the tall canopy bed and fireplace in her bedroom.

After an hour, Ralph Winston rounded everyone up. "Come into the den," he said, pointing to the window. "Do you see what I see?"

"It's snowing!" Benny said.

Big flakes drifted to the ground. "How beautiful!" Violet said.

"You promised you'd tell us the story of Madge Carson and Penelope on a snowy day," Jessie said. "Will you, Mr. Winston?"

"Ralph," he corrected. "Call me Ralph." He limped toward the den. "Yes, telling Madge's story is exactly what I had in mind. That's why I wanted all of you together.

"Madge Carson and her little girl, Penelope, lived in Trenton, New Jersey," Ralph began, sinking into an easy chair by the window as the children gathered around, sitting cross-legged at his feet. "Across the Delaware River from them was George Washington's army at Valley Forge."

"On Christmas Eve," he went on, "a few

British and paid German soldiers, called Hessians, were left to guard Trenton. Now, the troops planned a party and ordered Madge to bring them a dozen chickens. She knew that while the enemy partied it would be a perfect time for a surprise attack. Madge rowed across the icy river and told George Washington."

"Did General Washington fight the Hessians?" Violet asked.

"You bet he did! Washington and his soldiers crossed the river and trounced the astonished Hessians."

Betsy poked her head in. "I see you're still retelling Madge Carson's story." A tight little smile crossed her face. "No wonder. You've got a captive audience!"

"Hi, Betsy," Ralph said. "Want to join us?"

The slim young woman, dressed in boots, riding pants, and a plaid fitted jacket, held up her hand. "No, thank you. I came because of the leak in my bedroom ceiling. This new snow could crack the plaster."

"Find Larry. He'll fix it," Ralph said,

wrinkling his brow. "I'm busy."

"Hmmmf! If it was up to Larry he'd re-plaster — and repaint — all these old walls," Betsy said. She left, shaking her head.

"Now, where was I?" The old man tugged on his ear.

"What happened to Madge Carson?" Henry asked.

"When the Redcoats discovered Madge was missing, they knew she had spied on them," Ralph said.

"Redcoats were British soliders," Soo Lee announced, remembering what Henry had told her.

"Good for you!" Henry said, smiling at her.

"Madge dared not go home, so she ran into the woods. There, she hid, sheltering her little daughter against the cold."

"Poor Madge," Jessie said.

"Poor Penelope," Violet echoed.

"Madge avoided capture because she knew woodland trails and the river," Ralph continued. "Snow and cold made it hard to travel, especially with a small child. Finally, they arrived at Bennington, in what is now Vermont. Madge and Penelope were hid by the Ross family, original owners of Snowflake Inn."

"Did Madge and Penelope hide in the secret room?" Benny asked, his eyes round.

"When British troops arrived to search the inn, that's exactly where they hid," Ralph answered.

"I'll bet Penelope was scared," Soo Lee said in a small voice.

"They were both afraid," Ralph said, "but, with help, they managed to escape to Maine."

"That was an exciting story," Hannah said, her pretty face breaking into a smile.

"And to think it was a true one!" Henry said.

"Was Madge Carson the only one who hid in the secret room?" Davey asked.

"No, she wasn't," Ralph said. "During the Civil War several spies hid here. And Snowflake Inn hid slaves on the Underground Railroad."

"Underground Railroad?" Soo Lee asked,

"Did a train run under the ground?"

"No, no," answered Jessie, smiling. "In the Civil War, slaves who escaped from their owners were hidden by sympathetic people. The slaves were moved secretly from one house to another, all the way to Canada. This became known as the Underground Railroad."

"Oh, I see," Soo Lee said.

Later, when the sky darkened, Benny gazed out the window. "Is it time for our sleigh ride?" he asked impatiently.

"In a few hours," replied Jessie.

All at once, Greta stormed into the room, jabbing the air with a wooden spoon. "The stove won't work!" she said angrily, one hand planted on a hip. "If the stove doesn't work, neither do I!"

Oh, no, Henry thought. The horses are missing, the sink is cracked, the plaster's coming down, and now the stove is broken! What next?

CHAPTER 6

A Moonlight Sleigh Ride

Later that night, Benny was the first one ready to go on the sleigh ride. When he entered the den dressed in his warm jacket, cap, and mittens, Grandfather looked up from his book. "I see you're eager to go, Benny."

"Yes," Benny replied. "I can't wait, Grandfather. Why don't you come along on our sleigh ride?"

James Alden chuckled. "Thanks, Benny, but I'm comfortable sitting here by the fire. You go ahead and have a good time!"

"Oh, I will." Benny gave him a big smile. "We'll have a great time!" With a wave, he dashed off to join the others, who were waiting by the front door.

Ralph Winston clapped Davey on the back. "I'll hear all about your ride in the morning. Have fun, children!"

"Wouldn't you like to come along?" Violet asked.

Ralph shook his head. "No," he replied. "I'm going to turn in early."

"Then we'll see you tomorrow," Jessie said, opening the door. She was glad Ralph was going to bed. He worked hard and looked very frail. Clearly, he wasn't well and needed rest.

"Hurry up, Davey!" Benny yelled. "I'll race you to the stable."

The two boys tore down the path, and arrived breathless just as Larry hitched the horses to the sleigh. Dobbin and Robin snorted and stamped. As Larry fastened bells to the bridles, the horses blew out their breaths in white puffs.

While the boys clambered aboard, Jessie,

Violet, and Hannah petted the horses. Noticing the snow underfoot, Jessie said to Violet, "These are Larry's footprints!"

In the brightness of the yard light, Violet stooped, peering at the ground. "Yes, Larry's boot leaves an imprint of a horseshoe in the heel. But I can't believe Larry would have let the horses out. He's too nice."

"Let's keep our eyes open. Maybe someone else has the same heel design," Jessie suggested.

"Yes, I'm sure it's a popular pattern," Violet said. Yet, she remembered Larry's fight with his dad.

"Come on, everybody," Larry said, smiling, "into the sleigh!"

Once the children were settled on the side benches, Larry lightly touched the horses with the reins, and they pranced forward.

Violet said, "What fun!" She gazed about at the snow-covered fir trees. Big flakes continued to fall softly over everyone.

Rounding a curve, bells tinkled and horse hooves clip-clopped in the silent night.

"It's a fairyland," Henry said.

All at once Benny gave a gleeful yelp. He began to sing. "Jingle Bells, jingle bells, jingle all the way." Laughing, everyone else sang, too. "Oh, what fun it is to ride in a one-horse open sleigh!"

They sang and laughed for mile after snowy mile.

After an hour, Larry headed back to Snowflake Inn. When they'd almost reached the stable, Larry slowed and almost stopped.

"What's wrong?" Davey asked.

Larry chuckled. "Do you see what I see?"

Jessie craned her neck. A fat porcupine waddled across the road.

"I've never seen a porcupine before," Davey said, watching until the animal had disappeared into the woods.

"I have," Benny said proudly. "Once we helped a friend straighten out his mixed-up zoo."

Davey's eyes widened, impressed. "You did?"

Back at the inn, the children chattered and laughed all the way inside where they removed their jackets.

"Hi," Betsy called. "Did you have fun?"

"Yes, lots of fun," Violet said.

Hannah and Davey went upstairs, and the Aldens entered the living room.

Betsy, curled up in an easy chair with her stocking feet under her, put down her magazine. She'd placed her boots by the footstool. One boot had toppled over.

Henry stared at the boot. A horseshoe, outlined in the heel of the boot, could be seen clearly.

Betsy rose and stretched, running her hand through her blonde hair. "Hi, Cousin," she said to Larry, who came into the room.

"Hi, Betsy," Larry said, his lips pressed together. He held a piece of paper.

"How about a cup of coffee?" Betsy asked, picking up her boots.

"I could use one," Larry admitted. "Dad left me a note, asking me to fix the rusty pipe in my bathroom. That could take all night!" As he and Betsy left the room, Larry said, "I don't see why he won't just put in completely new plumbing! This old inn isn't going to last long at this rate! Someone is going to have to do something."

Betsy laughed. "You'll never change Uncle Ralph!"

Once Larry and Betsy were in the kitchen, Henry, leaning against the fireplace mantel, said, "Did anyone else notice Betsy's boot?"

"No, why?" Jessie asked.

"The heel had a horseshoe pattern," he replied.

Violet said, "Well, we know Larry's boots also have that same horseshoe design."

"Yes, we saw it again tonight in the snow," Jessie said.

"Larry acts like this is *his* inn," Henry said. "He wants to change all kinds of things around here." He dropped down onto the footstool.

Henry said, "Betsy might want Snowflake Inn for herself, too!"

"Yes," Jessie agreed. "She's Ralph's niece. He might let her take over the inn."

Yes, Jessie thought, both Betsy and Larry stood a good chance to inherit the inn. Were they trying to make so much trouble that Ralph would give up the inn now?

CHAPTER 7

Fire and Smoke

In the morning, after a hearty breakfast, the Aldens dressed to go ice skating. Davey and Hannah stood in the hallway. Henry noticed some soot on Hannah's sweater. "What happened?" he asked.

"Oh, Davey and I were just playing around near the fireplace and I fell down," Hannah explained.

"Would you like to come skating with us?" Violet asked.

"We didn't bring our ice skates," Davey said in a glum tone.

"I know what we'll do!" Benny said with a big smile, "I'll skate a while and then you can borrow my ice skates, Davey."

"That's a good idea, Benny," Jessie said. "We'll take turns."

"Hannah, my skates will fit you," Violet said. "We'll miss you if you don't come along."

"You will?" Hannah said in surprise.

"Yes, we will," Soo Lee said, giving them a little smile.

Pleased, Davey and Hannah hurried to get their jackets.

"Did I hear a pair of ice skates were needed?" Larry asked, coming into the room. His hair was messy, dark circles underlined his eyes, and his denim shirt was dirty. "Davey, you can use my old pair. I discovered them in the basement." He added angrily, "Where I've been all night, patching a crack in the boiler. I'm the number one repairman around here!"

His old friendly smile returned. "So, lucky for you, Davey, I ran across the ice skates I owned when I was your age." He turned as

Ralph entered the room. "Oh, good morning, Dad."

"Good morning, everyone," Ralph answered. "Is the boiler fixed, Larry?"

"I think it might last another week or so," Larry said in a cool tone.

Ralph shook his head. "I suppose I'd better order a new one."

"Of course, you should!" Larry snapped. "If the boiler breaks and floods the basement we'll have a real mess on our hands!" He turned and headed for the basement.

Ralph glanced at the children, then went over to a chair, sank down wearily, and rubbed his forehead.

Ralph looked ready to give up on Snowflake Inn, Henry thought. Maybe that was why he didn't seem in a rush to order a new boiler.

When Larry returned, he handed Davey his skates.

On the way to the pond, Violet walked beside Hannah. "Don't worry, Hannah. You can wear my skates most of the time. I want to sketch the ice skaters."

"Thanks," said Hannah. "That's really nice of you."

Arriving at the pond, the children laced up their ice skates. Violet sat on the side sketching the pond.

Jessie skimmed onto the ice, doing a spin or two.

"Jessie's like a real ice skater!" Davey said.

"She sure is!" Benny replied. "Jessie can skate backward, go fast, and do spins!"

"Where did she learn to skate so fancy?" Hannah asked, clearly admiring Jessie's grace and agility.

"From a professional ice skater," Henry explained, standing up. "You see, an ice skating troupe performed in Greenfield. We became friends with them."

"Alex was one of the stars and a wonderful skater," Violet added. "She taught Jessie different moves. She said Jessie was a natural."

Benny tottered out on the ice, then unsteadily skated to the other side of the small pond. "Coming, Davey?" he shouted.

Davey pulled his cap down over his ears and skated to Benny's side.

Jessie glided around the edge of the pond, then did a perfect pirouette in the center.

"Beautiful, Jessie," Violet called. "Do that again! I want to sketch you."

Soo Lee skated to Henry, and grabbed his hand. Henry laughed, motioning Hannah to join them. Soon all the skaters formed a line, hanging on to each other's waists. With Henry as the leader they zoomed around the pond. When the wind blew off Benny's cap, he laughed with glee.

Soon Hannah skated to the edge of the pond. "Violet, it's your turn to skate."

Shaking her hand, Violet said, "No, thanks, I want to finish this drawing."

So for the rest of the morning Hannah and the others skated, often stopping to pose for Violet.

"Hey!" Larry yelled as he arrived, standing up in the sleigh pulled by Robin and Dobbin, "how about a ride back to the inn? Greta has hot apple cider waiting for you!"

Eagerly the children removed their skates and climbed aboard the sleigh. They were ready for the warm inn and a hot drink.

Ralph, looking rested and happier, said as they arrived, "How about a fire, children?"

"Oh, could we?" Benny asked, his face shining.

"You bet!" Ralph answered. He bent down to Soo Lee. "Would you like a fire?"

"Yes, I would," Soo Lee said, looking up at Ralph with big, dark eyes.

Ralph chuckled, and with creaky knees, he kneeled on the hearth of the brick fireplace. "I've ordered a new boiler," he said matter-of-factly, "so nothing else should go wrong." He lit a match to the papers beneath the logs, and flames shot up the chimney.

In a short time smoke filled the room.

Jessie coughed and Violet held her hand over her nose and mouth. Tears welled up in Benny's eyes. "What's wrong with the fire?" he asked in a choked voice.

Ralph's eyes watered, too, as he used the poker to push aside the wood. Pouring water over the flames, he tried to extinguish the fire. Waving to the children and holding a handkerchief over his face, he wheezed,

"Children, go into the kitchen."

As the children left the room with their eyes watering, they met Larry who immediately took in the situation. He rushed to his father's side and helped put out the smouldering embers.

In the kitchen, Henry opened a window and Hannah opened the back door. The children huddled around the kitchen table. Benny sighed. They were having such a good time, and then this had to happen.

Larry, his face streaked with soot, entered the kitchen. "The fire's out!" he announced.

"What caused the smoke?" Violet questioned.

"Would you believe the chimney had been stuffed with rags and an old coat?" Larry said. "The smoke couldn't escape."

"Who would want to suffocate us?" Violet asked.

"I wish I knew," Larry said, pressing his lips together.

Henry recalled that Larry's clothes had been all dirty earlier. Maybe the dirt wasn't just from fixing the boiler. Then again, Hannah's sweater had been sooty. Could she and Davey be to blame?

Grandfather and Betsy came in the back door. "What has happened to you?" Grandfather asked. "You all look as if you've been crying!"

"We have!" Benny said in a loud voice. "But we're okay now."

"Grandfather, the chimney was stopped up," explained Jessie. "The den filled with smoke!"

"Is everything all right now?" Mr. Alden asked with concern, resting a hand on Henry's shoulder.

"Yes, it's fine now," Larry said. "We let plenty of fresh air in."

"Oh, dear," Betsy wailed. "I feel awful. Here I was out horseback riding, breathing in cold winter air."

Jessie gave Betsy a look. She wondered if Betsy really felt as badly as she said she did.

CHAPTER 8

Rustlings in the Night

On the fourth day of the Alden vacation, Henry rose early to help Larry clean the stable and curry the horses. He loved horses and was glad he could be around them.

On the way to the stable, Henry asked Larry, "Do you have any idea who would clog the chimney?" Secretly, he wondered if it might be Larry himself. If Larry couldn't get his way and modernize the inn, maybe he was deliberately trying to mess things up.

"I haven't a clue," Larry answered. "But

I know one thing! That coat didn't get up the chimney by itself!" He gave Henry a sideways look. "It could be those kids, Davey and Hannah. They're so bored, they might do anything for a little excitement."

Larry handed Henry an apple. "Give this treat to Dobbin. He'll be your friend for life."

Entering the stable, Henry sniffed the smell of hay and horses. What a pleasing odor — much better than Betsy's jasmine perfume!

Larry and Henry worked well together. The stalls were cleaned and the horses brushed before breakfast.

At the breakfast table, Violet asked, "Where is Grandfather?"

"He went along with Dad and Mr. and Mrs. Miller, to the antiques fair in town," Larry said.

"I wonder what Greta cooked today," Benny said, licking his lips.

Greta, carrying a platter of pancakes and bacon, said, "Well, Benny, does this answer your question?"

"Oh, boy! Pancakes!" Benny said. He rubbed his stomach. "I love pancakes!"

Soon, the heaping platter was empty.

"Now, what can we do?" Davey asked in a bored tone.

Betsy entered, and reached across the table, taking a banana from the fruit bowl in the center.

Jessie, glancing about, said, "You know, this old inn needs holiday spirit!"

"I know," Violet said. "The wreath on the front door is all the decoration there is."

"We can put up pine boughs!" Jessie suggested.

"And string popcorn," Henry added.

"Why don't you children come into town with me this afternoon," Greta said. "Mr. Winston has given me money for groceries and other things. You children can buy some decorations and spruce up Snowflake!"

"Yes!" Soo Lee said. "We'll make the inn pretty."

"Then it's settled," Greta said, her arms crossed. "After lunch we go to town."

Betsy wrinkled her nose in disgust. "No

matter how hard you try, you can't make this place attractive."

"Wait and see," Violet said with a smile. Why, she wondered, was Betsy always so sour wherever the inn was concerned?

Benny to the hall, lifting his jacket off a peg. "I'm collecting pinecones," he announced.

"Good idea! Let's go for a hike in the woods and as we walk we'll gather pinecones and holly," Jessie said, tying a wool scarf around her neck.

"Okay," Davey said half-heartedly. "At least it's *something* to do!"

"I'm ready," Henry said, putting on ear-muffs, and opening the door.

The children trudged through the snow and into the pine woods. Benny dashed ahead, scooping up snow and letting it drift over his face. "I love winter!" he shouted, his words echoing through the trees.

"Look!" Jessie called, plowing through a drift to a bush. "Holly bushes!"

Hannah, who had brought a pail, joined her. Soon everyone was gathering bunches

of holly and pinecones. Henry broke off a few pine boughs for the mantel in the den.

The morning flew by. When the children returned to Snowflake Inn, they carried a bucketful of pinecones and armfuls of fir branches and holly.

Later, after lunch, Greta drove them to town in the station wagon, and pulled up before a large discount store. The children spilled out, eager to buy decorations while Greta went on to the grocery store.

Going down the aisles of the store the children located holiday items. Jessie picked out red and green candles, and Benny and Soo Lee selected candy canes. Hannah and Violet chose crimson and green ribbons, Davey picked out some tinsel, and Henry found a large wreath.

Back at the inn, the children began to decorate. Jessie popped corn, then with Davey's help, strung it on a gold cord along with some cranberries Greta had bought. Violet and Hannah framed the front door with the popcorn and cranberry strings. Henry arranged pine boughs and red candles in the middle of the dining-room table. The large wreath was hung above the fireplace in the den by Jessie. Soo Lee and Benny strewed holly and pinecones on the mantel.

"Look what I've got, Benny," Henry said, holding up a sprig of mistletoe.

Benny's eyes grew big. "Where does that go?"

"Above the door going into the den," Henry answered, standing on a chair and fastening the mistletoe to the door beam.

"What's it for?" Benny wanted to know.

"Anyone standing under this gets a kiss."

Benny covered his mouth with his hand, giggling. "That's mushy stuff. You won't catch me under any old mistletoe!"

"Dinner!" Greta called.

"We need to finish," Benny replied.

"After you've eaten, you can go back to work," Greta said.

So after dinner the decorating continued. For an hour the children bustled from one room to another. When they were done, and the candles were lit and a cozy fire burned in the fireplace, the children stood back and admired their work. Snowflake Inn looked as warm and festive as the children felt.

When Grandfather and the others returned from the fair, their *ohs* and *ahs* made the children happy. They had worked hard, and were pleased that their holiday trimmings were appreciated.

That night, snuggled beneath the covers, Violet fell sound asleep. But around midnight, she awakened, hearing a strange rustling. "Jessie," she whispered, not wanting to wake Soo Lee.

"Ummmm," Jessie murmured, rolling over.

The rustling noise became louder.

Violet's heart thumped and she could hardly breathe. "Jessie!" she urgently whispered, shaking her. "Listen! Someone's in our room!"

CHAPTER 9

Greta Quits!

Jessie awoke with a start. "What's wrong, Violet?"

"Shhh, listen," Violet answered.

Jessie tilted her head. Sure enough, the sound of rustling papers came from the corner. Quietly, Jessie threw back the covers and switched on the desk lamp. Violet, sticking close to her side, followed.

"No one's here," Jessie said, peering around the room.

"Shall we check the closet?" Violet questioned.

Jessie shook her head. Putting a finger to her lips, she advanced on the wastebasket. All was silent. Suddenly, papers stirred in the wastebasket. Jessie pointed downward.

"What's in there?" Soo Lee said, rubbing her eyes and peeping inside the basket.

In her bare feet, Jessie crept toward the corner, reaching for her umbrella.

Violet took a lamp and held it close to the basket, while Jessie poked about in the papers.

"Squeak! Squeak!"

Jessie glanced back at Violet and smiled.

Violet bent nearer. She smiled, too. "Why, it's a sweet little field mouse."

Jessie scooped up the furry mouse, cupping it in her hands. "Let's put it outside so it will find its way back to its nest."

Violet opened the bedroom door and the three girls tiptoed downstairs.

"How would a field mouse find its way upstairs and into our wastebasket?" Violet said in a puzzled tone. "It seems more likely it would have been poking around in the kitchen, where there's food."

"You're right," Jessie answered. "Maybe someone deliberately put the mouse in our room to scare us."

Opening the front door, Violet felt cold air rush over her. Jessie gently placed the mouse on the doormat.

With a last squeak, the mouse dashed toward freedom and home.

"I heard the front door open," Henry said, coming down the steps, trailed by a sleepy Benny.

"We opened the door for a mouse," Jessie replied.

"A real mouse?" Benny asked, becoming wide awake.

"A real mouse," Violet replied with a smile. Then she related the story of the mouse in the wastebasket.

"I wish it had been in our wastebasket," Benny said, a wistful look on his face. Then he brightened. "Know what? I'm hungry."

"What a surprise," Henry said.

"How about a snack?" Jessie said.

"But Greta keeps the kitchen locked," Soo Lee said.

"Greta left a jar of cookies in the den," Violet suddenly remembered.

"Ummmm, yes," Benny said eagerly, hurrying into the den.

Sitting on the sofa in front of the cold fireplace, Violet said, "We think somebody put the mouse in our room."

"Why would someone do that?" Benny asked.

"Maybe to frighten us," Jessie said, pausing as she reached for a cookie. "Maybe someone wants us out of here for some reason."

Benny took a big bite of his chocolate chip cookie. "A little mouse isn't going to make us leave!"

Chuckling, Henry replied, "That's right, Benny. Some people, though, are afraid of mice and might have screamed." He glanced fondly at his sisters. "Whoever it was didn't know Violet and Jessie."

"A lot of things are happening that shouldn't be happening." Jessie rested her chin on her hand, thinking, "Remember the soot on Hannah's sweater the morning the chimney was clogged? Maybe Hannah and Davey left the mouse as a prank."

"Both Larry and Betsy had a horseshoe pattern — we saw it on their boot heels," Violet pointed out. "One of them might want to get the guests to leave."

"Maybe both of them," Henry said. "They could be in this together."

"I don't know," Jessie said. "My head is spinning."

"Let's go to bed," Violet said. "Tomorrow we'll see things in a clearer light."

The Aldens slept soundly that night and were in a good mood until they got downstairs. From the kitchen came the banging of pots and pans. All at once, Greta flung open the door. "The stove is broken again! And someone pulled out the refrigerator plug and ice cream has melted all over!"

"Not more troubles," Henry said.

"Yes, *more*," Greta replied. "And I keep the kitchen door locked at night, so I don't know how anyone got in, either."

"I'll repair the stove," Ralph soothed. "Don't worry, Greta."

"I'm not waiting!" Greta shouted, removing her apron and throwing it on a chair. "I quit!"

"Now, Greta," Ralph began, "we — "

But before he could finish his sentence, Greta stalked to the closet and struggled into her coat. Storming out, she slammed the door after her.

"Greta's gone," Ralph muttered, dropping into a chair. His face was gray with disappointment. "Since the stove isn't working, I'm afraid there won't be any hot breakfast. Day after tomorrow we were to have our big holiday dinner. Looks like you were right, Larry. I should modernize the inn." He shook his head. "Everything is going wrong!" He glanced up with sad eyes, looking at the Millers and James Alden. "I'll refund your money."

The stunned children stared at Ralph. Benny grabbed Grandfather's hand. Was their vacation at Snowflake Inn over so soon?

CHAPTER 10

Broken Glass

James Alden looked at the sad faces of his grandchildren, then turned to Ralph Winston and said, "We're staying!"

The Aldens shouted, "Hooray!"

"We'll stay, too," Mrs. Miller said, looking at her husband who nodded in agreement.

"Wonderful," Ralph said. "But how can we cook without a stove?"

"I have an idea," Grandfather said. "Will you allow me to buy a new stove?"

"That's very kind of you." Ralph sighed.

"But a new stove will ruin the look of our colonial kitchen."

Grandfather said, "Trust me, Ralph. I have an idea. Just tell me where I can find an appliance store."

"But who will cook our big dinner?" Ralph questioned.

"We will!" the Aldens chorused.

"And maybe Davey and Hannah can help," Violet suggested.

"But I don't know how to cook," Davey protested.

"Neither do I," Hannah said.

"Don't worry," Henry said. "You can cut up onions and celery, can't you?"

"I guess so," Davey replied.

Hannah brightened. "We'll help."

"Then that's settled," Grandfather said, his eyes twinkling. "I have a suggestion. Let's take the van and go into town for breakfast!"

"I'll take the jeep," Larry said reluctantly. "Mr. and Mrs. Miller, why don't you ride with me? We'll meet at Minnie's Coffee Shoppe."

"Where's Betsy?" Jessie asked.

"My niece is horseback riding," Ralph said. "She'll be back soon, but I know she wouldn't care to join us."

Just then Betsy breezed in, her blonde curls tousled and her cheeks rosy.

"Betsy," Larry said, "how about breakfast in town with us?"

She hesitated, then lifted her chin. "No, thank you." She ran upstairs, but in a minute she rushed downstairs. "My room!" she shouted. "It's freezing in there!" She glared at Larry. "The window is smashed and there's broken glass all over."

"How did that happen?" Ralph asked.

"I have no idea," Betsy said, looking suspiciously at Larry. "Someone must have been trying to break into my room from the balcony."

"We'll pick up the glass and I'll buy a new pane in town," Larry said with a sigh.

"Poor Betsy," Violet said.

Betsy stared at Violet for a minute, as if she couldn't believe Violet would sympathize with her. Then, with a toss of her head, she went into the den.

Henry accompanied Larry upstairs and they swept up pieces of glass and fitted cardboard in the window.

On the way to Minnie's Coffee Shoppe, Benny said, "We'll have turkey for our big dinner, won't we?"

"We must have turkey for dinner," Davey said, a worried expression on his freckled face.

"We'll definitely have turkey!" Violet said, smiling at the two boys.

After a hearty breakfast of eggs, bacon, and toast, Ralph visited the barber shop, Grandfather went to buy a stove, Larry took Steven and Rose Miller to view a historic mansion, and the children bought groceries for lunch and dinner.

Afterward, Hannah and Davey went to meet their parents while the Aldens stopped at a drugstore for hot chocolate.

"I don't believe Betsy is guilty of all those mean things," Violet said. "Not after her window was broken."

Henry pushed his empty cup aside. "I'm not so sure."

"Why?" Jessie asked. "Betsy's window was broken. She wouldn't break it herself, would she?"

"Well, it's funny," Henry continued, leaning back in his chair. "If a burglar stood on the balcony and broke the window, most of the glass would be *inside* Betsy's bedroom. But we cleaned up most of the pieces *outside*, on the balcony."

"You mean that someone must have broken the glass from *inside* the house?" Jessie asked.

"Right," Henry answered. "Also, I didn't see any footprints on the balcony."

"I hope Betsy isn't doing bad things to Snowflake Inn," Soo Lee said, her dark eyes worried.

Jessie said, "Remember how Betsy glared at Larry? She must think he's the guilty one."

"Maybe he is," Violet said.

Henry, glancing at his watch, jumped up. "We're late. We have to meet Mr. Winston. Grandfather told me he'd meet us back at the inn."

When they arrived at the inn, Grandfather

was there with a big smile on his face. "Come into the kitchen," he said.

Curious, Benny rushed into the kitchen. "Wow!" he exclaimed.

Ralph Winston moved forward, running his hand over the surface of the new stove. "Why," he said in amazement, "this stove looks more like an antique than the one taken out of here." Clearly, he was pleased.

"It looks like an antique, but cooks and bakes like a modern stove." Grandfather chuckled. "You see, Ralph? You can modernize this inn and it won't lose its eighteenth-century character."

Ralph's mouth set in a stubborn line. "This stove is change enough! I don't want any more modern things to ruin Snowflake!"

"Why are you so obstinate, Dad?" Larry said, his voice rising. "Maybe you should give up the inn."

Jessie, sensing another argument, interrupted in a cheerful tone, "How about letting us cook lunch on the new stove?"

"Sounds great," said Grandfather.

That afternoon, the children each scooped

up a big bowl of fresh snow, then drizzled maple syrup over it for a treat. While eating the delicious sweet, they planned their holiday menu. Later, Larry drove the Aldens into town to buy groceries for the big feast.

After dinner, the children gathered around the piano in the den. Jessie played, and everyone, in loud, happy voices, sang "Over the River and Through the Woods."

Henry brought in an armful of firewood. Attempting to light the fire, though, he leaped up in dismay. "This wood!" he shouted angrily. "It's wet! It was fine this afternoon. I checked it!"

"You mean someone poured water over it?" Benny asked, frowning. "Just so we couldn't have a fire?"

"That's ridiculous!" Larry growled, throwing down a log in disgust. "No one would do that."

Violet's heart picked up a beat. Who was doing all these mean things? Was it Betsy? Or Larry? Why wouldn't they stop?

CHAPTER 11

Benny and the Secret Room

"So what if the firewood is wet!" Jessie exclaimed. "Who needs a fire?" She jumped up from the piano. "I have an idea. Let's bake holiday cookies!"

"Yes, yes," Benny responded. "We'll have a good time tonight."

"We can try out the new oven," Violet pointed out.

"Good idea," Henry said. "The oven needs testing before we roast the turkey tomorrow."

The children trooped into the kitchen,

bringing out cookie sheets and cookie cutters. Jessie preheated the oven.

Henry mixed sugar cookie dough, Violet rolled it out, and Davey and Benny cut out stars, bells, and candy canes.

Then Jessie mixed up dough for a batch of Russian tea balls. When her cookies were baked, Benny, Soo Lee, and Davey rolled them in powdered sugar. Next, they decorated some of the sugar cookies with red and green gum drops, others with sparkly candies.

The children topped the evening off by eating warm cookies and drinking cold milk. Bedtime arrived before they knew it.

Tucking himself in, Benny refused to think about all the bad things that had happened. Surely, nothing else bad would take place. Instead, he thought about the holiday feast the following evening. What fun it would be to cook the dinner. With happy thoughts of pumpkin pie and whipped cream, Benny drifted off to sleep.

In the morning the kitchen became a flurry of cooking activity as the children prepared the turkey, simmered the giblets, and boiled cranberries and sugar.

Rose Miller entered, surveying the busy kitchen. "May I give you a hand?"

"No, Mother," Hannah answered with a smile. "We've got everything under control."

"Well, all right," Rose said doubtfully. "But, please let me know if you need help." She backed out. "If you're sure you don't need me, your dad and I will go for a walk."

" 'Bye, Mom," Davey said, smiling and waving. "We'll be fine. The Aldens are showing us what to do."

Rose smiled, too. She seemed pleased that Hannah and Davey were helping in the kitchen and clearly enjoying themselves.

The Aldens turned back to their chores.

Davey and Soo Lee chopped onions for the stuffing. Benny diced celery. In a big bowl, Violet tore up pieces of bread, mixing in an egg, and Jessie simmered chicken broth to pour over it. Soo Lee sprinkled the mixture with salt, pepper, and sage. Hannah stirred the ingredients together. Next, Jessie and Benny stuffed the turkey cavity with the moist dressing.

Finally, Henry carried the roaster, with the twenty-pound turkey in it, to the oven and placed it inside.

"Hey, kids," Larry said, poking his head in, "let's take a sleigh ride down to the pond. You can help me feed the ducks and geese."

"Oh, boy!" Benny said. "Let's go."

"I thought most birds had flown south for the winter," Jessie said.

"These birds are on their way," Larry said with a chuckle, "but we can fill their stomachs so they'll have a good flight."

Violet thought it couldn't be Larry. He was too nice.

The sleigh ride reddened the children's cheeks and put big smiles on their faces.

When they arrived at the pond, a flock of geese had landed on the shore. Benny and Davey raced ahead, each with a bag of bird seed. After scattering the seed over the ground, the two boys were delighted to see the honking geese devour the food.

Violet and Henry, carrying seed, moved to another area where mallard ducks had settled.

Soo Lee fed a lone duck by an oak tree. Hannah and Jessie helped Larry unload a huge sack of feed and distribute it along the edge of the pond.

After the birds had been fed, the children climbed aboard the sleigh for the ride back to the inn.

"I hope nothing has happened to the turkey or cranberry sauce," Violet said. The way things had been going, she wasn't sure what they'd find next!

"Grandfather and Ralph will protect the kitchen," Jessie said reassuringly.

Overhearing these remarks, Benny jumped up and down on the bench. "Go faster, Larry!"

From an easy trot, Dobbin and Robin broke into a gallop and soon the children were back in the kitchen, pleased to find that everything was as they'd left it. They quickly prepared a late breakfast of cinnamon toast and oatmeal.

Davey rang the bell to announce that breakfast was ready, and everyone assembled around the dining-room table.

"We'd better not eat too much," Benny said. "We need to have a big appetite for our holiday dinner." Benny grinned at Betsy.

Betsy pushed aside the oatmeal. "I only wanted toast," she said.

Betsy's perfume tickled Benny's nose. He sneezed. "Ah-choo!"

Betsy rose and smiled suddenly. "I'll help you make the dinner. Then I'm going horseback riding."

The children were all pleased with Betsy's offer of help and her good spirits.

After eating, the children and Betsy cleared the table, and set to work making biscuits, mashed potatoes, scalloped corn, candied yams, apple salad, and pumpkin pies.

Benny, who had been cutting up walnuts for the apple salad, sneezed again. "I'm going upstairs for a tissue," he said.

Jessie laughed. "Betsy's jasmine perfume makes you sneeze."

"I'm sorry," Betsy said. "I'll go riding now and you'll stop sneezing."

"I'll be back to help," Benny promised, hurrying to the steps.

On the way there, however, he slowed his steps, remembering the secret room. Maybe clues were hidden in there and he could be the one to find the mystery person. He was tired of the mean tricks.

Standing before the brick wall, Benny pushed one brick, then another, but the door didn't budge. At last, he pressed the right brick and the door swung open. Carefully, he inched forward. He'd only advanced a few steps, however, when the door clicked shut! Benny, his heart thudding, tried to see in the blackness. Now he was locked in the secret room and no one knew where he was! What should he do? Benny sank to the floor and put his head in his hands. What if he was in this dark, scary place forever?

CHAPTER 12

The Guilty One

Inside the secret room, Benny wrinkled his nose, lifting his head. Jasmine! Betsy's perfume followed him everywhere, even here. Slowly, he moved about, unable to see.

What if he missed the holiday feast? He had to find a way out! His eyes were getting used to the dark and he saw, on one wall, a low, rounded door. When he twisted the handle, the door opened. On hands and knees, he emerged into the kitchen!

"Benny!" Violet called, pulling her

brother from under a worktable. "Where have you been?"

Henry leaned down, astonished. "Look how this wallpaper hides an opening in the wall. Where did you come from, Benny?"

"The secret room," Benny answered.

Jessie put her arm around his shoulders. "Poor Benny! You must have been scared."

"A little," he confessed in a low tone.

"Now we know how a person can get into Greta's locked kitchen," Henry said.

"And while I was in there I smelled *Betsy*'s perfume!" Benny said.

"Are you sure?" Soo Lee asked, dusting off a cobweb from Benny's shirt.

"Betsy must have been in there," Jessie said.

"But why would she creep around in that secret room?" Benny asked. "It's dark and scary."

"Well, if she was up to no good . . ." Henry began.

"And she didn't want anyone to know . . ." Violet added.

"I bet that's how she got into the locked kitchen to break the stove," Jessie said.

"What should we do?" Violet asked.

"Dinner's almost ready. I think we should wait until afterward before we do anything," Henry said.

"How are things going, children?" Grandfather said, as he came in just then. He sniffed. "Those pumpkin pies smell wonderful."

"We're right on schedule, Grandfather," Jessie said. "After we set the table, we'll take our baths and dress for dinner."

"Good, good," James Alden said. "I'm getting hungry."

"I *am* hungry!" Benny said.

Hannah smiled and turned to Violet. "I'm going to wear my new red dress," she said.

"I can't wait to see it," Violet answered, accompanying Hannah up the stairs.

Jessie and Henry followed.

Benny and Davey were last, staying behind to each dip a finger into the whipped cream for just a taste.

After the boys took their baths, they

slicked down their hair and pulled on their best sweaters.

The girls, already downstairs, were in the kitchen, dishing the food into bowls.

"Anything left for us to do?" Henry asked.

"Please take the turkey out of the oven," Jessie said. "Put it on the big platter, and set it at Grandfather's place for carving."

"Will do," answered Henry cheerfully.

"We're ready," Jessie pronounced, removing her apron.

Soo Lee rang the dinner bell.

When Steven and Rose Miller came in, Rose stepped back with a gasp. "How beautiful! How the crystal, silver, and china sparkle in the candlelight!"

Pleased, Henry smiled. All their hard work was appreciated. Down the center of the table bunches of holly, pine boughs, and pinecones surrounded six crimson candles. Clearly it was holiday time!

Grandfather sat at one end of the long table with the huge golden brown bird before him. At his left, Larry stared in amazement. "You kids have done a great job!" he marveled.

"I agree!" Ralph said, "I've never seen the dining room so festive and magnificent."

The smiling children stood in the doorway, admiring the table. Henry snapped a picture.

"Where's my niece?" Ralph asked, glancing about.

Soo Lee turned. But there was no Betsy!

Benny tugged on Jessie's sleeve, beckoning her to follow him. The other Aldens went along, too, trooping into the den.

Benny pointed to Betsy, who lay sobbing on the sofa.

"Betsy," Violet said, dashing forward and patting the young woman's shoulder. "What's wrong?"

Betsy continued to cry.

"What's wrong?" Benny repeated.

Betsy sat up. "It's all of you," she said between sobs.

Benny's eyes widened and he looked at Henry in bewilderment. Why was Betsy blaming them?

CHAPTER 13

Good-Bye, Snowflake Inn

"*Us?*" Jessie asked in disbelief. "What did *we* do?"

"Do? Why, you've been sweet and good to me," Betsy replied, "and I've repaid your kindness with meanness! I've done awful things! Things I'm ashamed of."

"You mean you released the horses?" Henry said.

Miserably, Betsy nodded.

"You stuffed up the chimney?" Davey asked.

Betsy nodded.

"You unplugged the refrigerator?" Soo Lee questioned.

Betsy nodded.

"You poured water over the firewood?" Violet said.

Betsy nodded.

"You broke the stove?" asked Benny.

Betsy nodded.

"You smashed your *own* window?" Jessie asked in surprise.

"Yes," Betsy whispered and hung her head. Tears trickled down her cheeks.

"Did you put the mouse in our room, too?" Violet asked.

"No! I didn't do that," Betsy said.

"Hey!" Ralph poked his head in. "What's the hold up?" When he saw Betsy, his smile became a frown. "What's wrong, dear?"

"Oh, Uncle Ralph, I must tell you something," Betsy murmured, wiping her eyes and blowing her nose. She rose.

Ralph, his face filled with concern, said, "What is it?"

Gently, Betsy guided her uncle into a big chair. Once he was sitting down, she confessed the awful things she'd done to the inn.

"But *why?*" Ralph asked.

"I wanted Larry to be blamed," she said between sniffles. "I thought if he were blamed, then I would inherit Snowflake Inn when you retired. I intended to sell it and open a restaurant in Philadelphia. I realize now how terrible I've been."

Uncle Ralph stood and put his arm around Betsy. "You've done some very bad things. But come into dinner, Betsy. We'll discuss this later."

When they arrived in the dining room, Grandfather was ready to carve the turkey.

The children sat down, relieved that, at last, the mystery had been solved.

Grandfather gave thanks for such a splendid dinner, then everyone heaped their plates with turkey, potatoes and gravy, dressing, cranberry sauce, corn, and candied yams.

"This is delicious," Steven Miller said.

"I peeled the potatoes," Davey piped up.

"And I baked these," Hannah said, passing a basket of biscuits.

"I'm proud of both of you," Rose said.

"Would you like to help me cook and bake when we get home?"

"Yes!" Davey and Hannah answered together.

After dinner, everyone helped clean up. Then the children sat in front of the kitchen fireplace.

"We're leaving at 5:30 in the morning," Hannah said. "I hate to go."

"We're sorry to see you go, too," Jessie said.

"I had a good time," Davey admitted, poking at the fire and watching the flames shoot up. "I didn't think I would."

"We both had fun," Hannah said. "I'm glad I came."

Henry said, "Davey, did you put a mouse in the girls' room?"

Davey looked guilty. "It was just a joke."

"It's all right, Davey," Jessie said. "We can take a joke."

Hannah turned to Violet. "Will you be my pen pal?"

"Oh, yes," Violet answered. "We'll write often!"

After they'd said good-bye, Jessie said, "I can't believe that I'd thought *they* were the troublemakers. They're really nice kids." The other Aldens agreed.

The next morning the Aldens rose early to pack and prepare breakfast. Hannah and Davey were already on their way back to Boston.

Betsy came into the kitchen. She poured a cup and sat at the kitchen table. "You know, Uncle Ralph forgave me! Everyone has been wonderful and I've been so rotten." She paused, sipping her coffee. "Uncle Ralph is going to help finance my restaurant, and I've promised to pay for all the damage I've caused."

"Was Larry angry?" Benny asked.

"Very angry," Larry said, coming in from the living room. "At first." He smiled at Betsy. "But I'm glad everything's out in the open and over, at last!"

"I hate myself for doing those things," Betsy said. "And you were so understanding."

"Hi, kids," Ralph said, entering the room. "Can you believe I'm hungry after our feast last night?"

Benny nodded. "I'm hungry, too."

"You know, Dad," Larry said, "I think you're right. Snowflake Inn is charming just the way it is."

Ralph winked. "We do need a phone, though. And a new boiler."

Chuckling, Larry gazed warmly at his father. "Do you think we've reached a compromise on our inn?"

"Guess so," Ralph answered. "If we each give a little, we'll have a mighty fine place."

After breakfast, the Aldens packed, then got in the car. As Grandfather pulled out of the drive, they all waved to Betsy, Larry, and Ralph, who stood in the doorway.

Grandfather gave a horn toot, and they were on their way back to Massachusetts!

It had been a great vacation, Jessie thought, leaning back on the seat. A vacation with a mystery. What could be better?

GERTRUDE CHANDLER WARNER discovered when she was teaching that many readers who like an exciting story could find no books that were both easy and fun to read. She decided to try to meet this need, and her first book, *The Boxcar Children*, quickly proved she had succeeded.

Miss Warner drew on her own experiences to write the mystery. As a child she spent hours watching trains go by on the tracks opposite her family home. She often dreamed about what it would be like to set up housekeeping in a caboose or freight car — the situation the Alden children find themselves in.

When Miss Warner received requests for more adventures involving Henry, Jessie, Violet, and Benny Alden, she began additional stories. In each, she chose a special setting and introduced unusual or eccentric characters who liked the unpredictable.

While the mystery element is central to each of Miss Warner's books, she never thought of them as strictly juvenile mysteries. She liked to stress the Aldens' independence and resourcefulness and their solid New England devotion to using up and making do. The Aldens go about most of their adventures with as little adult supervision as possible — something else that delights young readers.

Miss Warner lived in Putnam, Connecticut, until her death in 1979. During her lifetime, she received hundreds of letters from girls and boys telling her how much they liked her books.